THE KINGS OF ONE COLOR

RICHARD W. KELLY

THE KINGS OF
ONE COLOR

TITLES BY RICHARD W. KELLY
MEENDUK.COM

Bizarro
- ❖ The Cattercorns of Cloudville Arizona

Christian
- ❖ My Journey Into Christianity
- ❖ Noel Not an Angel: A Christmas Novella

Fantasy
- ❖ The Kings of One Color

Historical Fiction
- ❖ The Early Years of 'Squirt' Malone

Horror
- ❖ Testament

Short Stories
- ❖ Solundrums
- ❖ Solundrums V.2

Slice of Life Books
- ❖ The Cultural Phenomenon of Super Jam and the Tragedy Therein
- ❖ Lost Vegas, Nevada
- ❖ A Novella About Pie That Should Have Starred Jason Sudeikis
- ❖ Times... They Are A Changin'

Thriller
- ❖ The American Martyr
- ❖ The MARX Beasts

Young Adult
- ❖ The Psi-Chotic Adventures of Drew Darby

THANK YOU

I would like to thank my mom for continuing to read this week after week as I finished each chapter. Then not killing me once I got writers block and abandoned the story for three years.

Chapter 1

Impressions

The rubble of the trail bounced off of Patricka's shoes as she ran into the chapel looking for her father. The beauty of the building and the honesty of the tradition were lost on her as she made her way down the aisle of wooden pews. The image of all five kings of the world presiding over the globe overlooked the girl, but again she did not pay attention to the importance behind such a statue. She ignored the stained glass, the hanging torches, the alter, the Book, everything that a ten year old takes for granted when they live in a family with a priest as father.

She turned the corner, bounded up the steps and burst through the thick wooden door to reveal Moshe, her father, working on his next sermon. "Papa! I have news! I have news!"

Moshe slowly lifted his balding head to his daughter and suppressed a chuckle at her excitement. "Dear, is this how you enter the house of God? The workplace of your father? The monument of our great ruler?"

"Sorry Papa." Patricka quickly curtsied turning her focus

to one of the many Penta Diamonds attached to the walls of the wooden room. She mumbled random syllables at an inaudible level hoping her father would assume she recited a prayer. "My news!" She swiveled her orientation back to her father.

He held up a finger as he put a last few words to paper before he could move his attention to Patricka. His eyes slowly moved up from the paper to meet the young girl's. "Go."

"I received my calling!" Excitement burst from her face as if she were turning to steam.

It was news that should be considered a great achievement, but it was also news that Moshe had been dreading for the last four years when he first met his daughter. He closed his eyes to fight tears while letting a smile shine through to honor Patricka's achievement. He rose to his feet looking like a man ready to face execution. He straightened his spine coming to his full stature and made his way over to the panting girl and leaned over for a hug.

"Don't you want to know what I will be doing?" Patricka hugged her father back out of habit, but she could not hide the annoyance that he was not inquiring about her announcement.

Moshe held her tightly, a tear forming in the corner of his eye, "No, not now. You will from this point forward be a woman and in so you shall announce this as a woman would. We must have a feast tonight!"

Patricka pushed herself away from her father to bounce about the room displaying the sheer giddiness she possessed. She turned mumbling thanks to her dad and hopped back down the steps to go on with her day.

Moshe sighed in frustration at the fact that this moment had happened so soon. The king always gave children their calling, but most would not find out until they were nearly twenty years old. But, for Moshe, his daughter would begin her adult life and her training for her life's work at the young age of ten.

As he made his way out of his office and back down to the stone framed chapel he let his mind wander. It contemplated things that he was, of course, ashamed of questioning, but things that were only natural for his situation.

'Why did he choose her?' He thought to himself. 'When I was talking to the children of choice to pick my daughter, why did I have to pick Patricka? Why did I pick the child with the most promise?' The idea of having not picked her darkened his outlook briefly, but it was just a horrible fantasy. He picked her because she was the one. He felt a connection with her that no other child came close to providing for him. Unfortunately, the king had felt it was time she started doing God's work now.

Maybe it was his own connection with God that he chose her. Maybe the connection he felt was in actuality a connection between Patricka and God. Maybe he knew all along that his family would be torn apart quicker than most.

He turned back at the statue of the kings and the world before he left the chapel. He bowed to the image of the five kings and the Earth they presided over. The Penta Diamond hung there portraying the image so clearly. The world was overlooked by the five kings who were the only people in existence that had communication with God. It was the reason they were the only people who were represented inside the chapel. The symbolism was lost to some, but Moshe understood it, he had written sermons on it before.

He followed his religious practices. He bowed and thanked the black king while looking into the eyes of the statue within the black diamond. He bowed and thanked the yellow king while eyeing the face within the yellow diamond.

He did the same for the red king in the red diamond and the fat king in the grey diamond. He then touched his forehead, the metaphoric third eye, as he thanked the white king, his king, the ruler of his home lands, and gazed deeply into the visage of the man in the white diamond. Then he touched his heart and thanked God as he looked up at the ceiling of his chapel.

The stepped out of the building taking backwards steps letting the image of the statue make an impression on him. Letting the importance of everyone's attachment to God become visible to him, he breathed deep.

He closed the doors to the chapel.

Wyndsoria was frantic to get the preparations for her daughter's feast together. When Moshe had chosen her as the mother for their family, Patricka's calling had become the biggest event of her life.

When Wyndsoria was sixteen she received her calling from the white king. She remembered sitting in school, trying to understand the importance of avoiding progress, when a guard entered the class room with a note from the king.

Blessed be this day, the fourth of winter in the nine hundred eighty first year of their dynasty, the white king. You, Wyndsoria Wyndhaven have been called upon to serve your country, your fellow man, your king, and your God as a Water Bearer. In one day's time, you will travel to the town of Listerbourne to manage the water source for the community. Celebrate and pay homage to your God by devoting your life to this work.

When she held the note she shook with gratitude. The moment when she realized that God had a plan for her and he had told the king it was her time to work, was the most meaningful occasion of her life. But now, with her daughter of four years being called upon, the biggest experience of her life would be honoring Patricka.

Her hut was filled with smoke and steam as she prepared a feast. It was a lot of work to make a meal for the whole of their society, but this was her task and she would not fail for Patricka.

She had wanted the celebration to be a surprise to everyone in their village, but she had to tell the hunter to round up five hogs. And, she had to tell the farmer that it was necessary to use up three percent of their harvest for this one day. And, there was no avoiding telling the musician that he would be needed all night. But she still managed to keep it a secret from most.

She had managed to get three of the hogs over a single fire pit and only needed find one more pit to roast the other two. She had cut the onions and carrots for the soup and retrieved a couple gallons of water. That would be used to make the broth when the hogs would come off.

As the smoke began to burn her eyes, Wyndsoria stepped out of her hut to get some fresh air. The village was working its daily duties. The pebbled path in front of her home was freshly raked, the huts of the other families had been straightened back from the heavy winds of the morning. She could hear the patter of carriages being pulled by horses down the way. And the scent of the blacksmith just around the corner melting metals into the items he needed drifted across the entirety of the town.

Sometimes she wished she had been assigned to a richer community, but not that night. That night she was thankful for what she had and the passion everyone would show for Patricka. As she basked in the glory that would soon befall her daughter, Moshe walked up the trail. His head was low and his dark robes slowly gathered the light colored dust that plagued the small village.

Wyndsoria rushed over to embrace her husband, the duties of a wife, "Wonderful day! Our daughter has become a woman." Her words were what she knew she should feel, but they betrayed her true feelings about her daughter walking out of her life. He put his arms around one of the members of his house that was not leaving him in the next few days.

"I know you have been looking forward to this day. Maybe I should leave you to preparations and go get Ash from school?" Moshe tried to put a happy tone to his suggestion.

"Yes! Go get her brother. He must hear the news!"

Moshe kissed his wife on her smoke stained forehead and continued his trek through the town. He passed his hut and went down the trail towards the school. He was reminded of just yesterday when he was walking the trail to gather both his children, but now he did not know where his daughter was. But, it was no matter, she was no more his daughter now than anyone else's. She was another active member of society.

He imagined his Patricka going out to her new town, her new job, her new life and he wondered what it would be like. Moshe had the luxury of staying in his birth village. When he was called upon to spread the word of God he was taking over for his village's priest who had been sent away to the yellow king's land.

It was the way of commerce. The kings would barter with each other to gain new technology or fashion or entertainment by trading citizens between kingdoms. Luckily the former priest had no family left when he was traded. It was the way they did things. The best and brightest, it seemed, were traded away, but it was always those who were now alone, those who had no family to speak of.

The thought brought horror to Moshe. What if Patricka had been traded? What if the girl he had spent the last four years raising was being sent to the yellow king's land where she would become a savage like those who followed their barbarian king? But he pushed the idea aside. She had a family, it was not the way things worked.

He walked up to the school. It was a lone wooden building in the middle of their desert. It seemed calm while the classes were still in session, but once they let out he knew of the madness that would encompass the school yard. He enjoyed the silence as he kicked the rubble from the trail, allowing it to bounce off his religious robes.

There was not much time to dwell on the change in his life before the time had come for school to be dismissed. A faint rumble like that of an impending thunderstorm rolled across the ground as the children began to emerge from the building.

The sound thickened with each child that emerged from the doors. After a few minutes, Moshe saw Ash come out of the building frantically looking around.

Moshe rushed to him to ease his fear of his missing sister. "Over here!" He waved his arms wildly in an attempt to catch Ash's eye.

His son nodded at him and made his way over to his father, "I can't find Patricka."

"She is home." The words came out solemn.

"Is she ok? What could have happened while she was in class?" Fear and panic invaded the boy's speech.

"No. She has received her calling."

Shock. Ash's jaw dropped. "But, she is only ten. How could I not have been called first? I am sixteen." It was all mumble, but Moshe felt his son's despair.

"Let's walk home."

The village was buzzing with anticipation. Festivals of

this type were both a celebration as well as a somber goodbye party. It was almost unheard of for someone to stay with their village. Most people were sent to far away cities to serve a new community, to keep their emotions and attachments subdued while their obligation to God remained at the forefront.

Wyndsoria had prepared all five hogs, two gallons of soup, ten loaves of bread and ten pies. She was exhausted but glowing with excitement for the honors of her daughter. The light from the sun dimmed with the sunset and the community began to gather on the trail.

It was obviously a special occasion, the village as a whole almost never congregated. The people began to congregate and have meaningless conversations near their huts. The music of the pan flutist started soft, but gained intensity as people began to compete with it for their conversation volume.

Ash had gathered wood and stacked it for a bonfire in the center of the trail. As the sun dipped down past the horizon he brought out a torch and lit the bonfire in honor of his sister, Patricka.

The gleam from the fire shone on the people of the village making their grey skin almost shine. It was something they rarely noticed as nearly every person on the planet was a grey skin, but when they congregated in special light it came to prominence.

The pan flute rose in volume and a group of girls came out of one of the huts and began to dance. It was the dance of the Calling, a dance that all girls learned as soon as they could walk.

Patricka absorbed the honor as she realized that everything was put together in regard to her becoming a woman. She let the movement of the girls overtake their physical presence. In her view there was nothing more than motion.

When the dance had finished Moshe approached one of the hogs for the carving. He bowed his head and said a prayer, "Dear Lord, we thank you dearly from our humble village for allowing us the blessings we have gladly taken from you. We thank you for giving us the White King who allows us to hear your voice through his own. And we thank you for the honor you have bestowed upon Patricka who takes her steps now to becoming the woman you mean her to be." He stepped aside and motioned for Patricka to speak.

Patricka walked towards the smoking hog attempting to be graceful, but still looking like a child playing dress up. "Thank you. This is wonderful. I am scared, but happy. Today is my last day as a child and tomorrow I start my life as an information bearer." She giggled, and then cried.

Moshe reached for the knife letting his pride for his daughter shine through. He raised it ceremoniously to stab the hog when he noticed movement out in the darkness. His pause grasped the attention of the town. They all turned to the expanse past the fires where they could see three men approaching.

The shine of their armor told Moshe that it was the king's men coming for Patricka. "Welcome! We appreciate you arriving so swiftly to fetch your newest information bearer, but we are still celebrating Patricka's accomplishment. If you don't mind us finishing our ceremony." His voice echoed out into the nothingness as the clinking of the men's armor came into the area.

"Ho!" Said one of the men as the fire began to illuminate their pale skin. "We will happily let you finish your celebration, but you may want to make it for two."

The words rung deep sorrows into the community while the thick scent of the pork sting everyone's nostrils.

"We come for two. Patricka and we have a calling for

Ash." No matter how unthreatening the man's face was, it would be the face of Moshe's nightmares until he would see his children reunited with him again.

Ash pushed his way through the small crowd to meet the men and receive his calling. He showed no disdain for his calling coming during a celebration for his sister, he instead appeared to be a boy stealing a spotlight.

A whisper leaked from his mouth, "King's personal guard."

The crowd erupted and Patricka came over to hug her brother. Both of them were moving on with their lives together. As a guard and an information bearer they would be in the same city, the same city as the king, the city of Sodorrah.

Moshe handed the knife to his son acknowledging his transition into manhood and went to be next to his wife. Wyndsoria was crying as he approached her. She looked into his eyes with a pained smile and buried her face in his chest. Not because she loved him, not because it was her duty as his wife, but because she had no one else left. He patted the back of her head as he watched his two children gleefully accept the end of their childhood.

He watched them dance, eat, sing, talk, but eventually it faded from his sight as he reminisced about the life he experienced with them. He chuckled as he relived their days out of their pre-family houses.

Ash was such an athletic little six year old that they always said they knew who the birth parents were. Since it was assumed that most kids were physically born in their towns there were few people who could have given their genetics to such a strong little boy.

There was always more mystery with Patricka. Over the four years she was his daughter she never showed signs that she was birthed by anyone they knew. It might have been why she seemed so special to them. She was the most individual person Moshe had ever met.

As his eyes refocused on the celebration it became very clear that he was done with them. There were no more lessons, no more talks, no more hard times, everything was over and it was just him and his wife.

The night seemed to last for years, but they always did. The men from the king stayed and got to know Ash and Patricka as they were all headed to live in the same city. It was an odd coincidence that two people from one family were going to the same place, but it was a part of God's plan. Not even the king would have dared defy God's command.

Eventually, everyone went home and the night was over. Patricka and Ash spent their last night in their bed while Moshe and Wyndsoria spent it in their kitchen, awake and dreading the children's departure.

As the sun arose the next day it was a scene that had two sides. The children were moving onto the important work of their lives while the parents watched the greatest joy of theirs walk away forever. Wyndsoria retreated to her bed after she gave her final hugs and kisses, but Moshe went to work. The work of God did not stop for his own pain.

Chapter 2

Apprehension

Patricka left her home for the capital city of Sodorrah. She was truly excited about her new life, but the fact that she would be able to start it with her brother meant everything. She did not know what she was losing. Her childhood was cut short. She would not spend another morning playing tag or wishing for a present. From this point on she was an adult.

She tried her best to be grown up. She, Ash, and the three guards wandered out in the desert. They walked with a purpose. They walked to a beat. Except Patricka, she tried, but shortly after they started out she skipped alongside of the others unable to repress her young age.

"What's it like?" Her voice was nothing but childish fascination. Her eyes glittered with anticipation as she looked to the guard leading the way.

"What was that?" Obviously caught off guard by the question he looked back at her as he walked through the loose sand.

"Sodorrah. The city, the life, the job…" She hesitated as a goofy grin smeared across her face. "The king."

Ash groaned at the immaturity of his sister as the sun beat down on his pale grey face.

The guard laughed to himself. "You will see what it is like, but what you should be concerned with is your calling." He brushed some of the stray sand out of his facial hair as he looked to the horizon for the transportation depot.

"You will be an information bearer, a defensive information bearer to be specific. You are charged with all the knowledge that the king needs in regards to our defenses. That would include past, present and future. That is more important than what it is like to live in Sodorrah."

She sensed the condescension in his voice and out of youthful pride she tried to up-sell herself. "I am well aware of the history of mankind and all the defensive knowledge that goes along with it. I am aware of the heathens from millennia ago who defiled God with their electricity, gluttony, modified biology, and massively destructive weapons. I know everything there is to know about how God adorned his own heritage through the five kings! The black king, the yellow, the red king, the white king, and the fat king are the people of God and we are their servants in worship of the one true God, damn it!" She cringed as she cursed, but she felt she was in the right, she was an adult now.

The guard stopped in his tracks kicking up dirt from the abrupt end to his motion. "That is all peasant bullshit. You have a lot to learn and there is no time for errors now. You are in your calling. This is the work the king has put upon you as he heard from the lips of God himself." He turned back to his trek and muttered, "As you would put it.", and marched on.

The diatribe had put Patricka in her place. She may be technically a woman now, but the guard had just shown her that she had a lot to learn before she would be respected. She spent the rest of the journey in silence, sulking in her ten year old way. She let her mind grasp at the humiliation of the guard's words while her lungs warmed through with the searing desert heat.

After a couple hours of testing the stamina of their calves in the sinking sand of the desert dunes, they came over a hill and set their eyes upon the depot. It was a sight that was talked about among children and reminisced between adults. Anyone born outside of a main city never saw a transportation depot except for when they left for their calling.

The area was an ancient city with the remnants of square brick buildings, lines of flat concrete, and random wires sticking out from everywhere. There were lines of horses ready to take people to the east. There were guides prepared to walk people to their callings in the south and steel rails that would take Patricka and her brother north, to the city of Sodorrah where they would begin their adult lives.

They did a sideways walk down the final dune to the broken concrete grounds below. As they got closer they eyed the odd writings etched into the buildings. Strange symbols adorned small concrete squares set into the remaining bits of the bricked structures.

The entire thing felt like a portal into a past that they were trained to despise. It was a world they never knew and would never understand. Just seeing the writings of the lost past felt like blasphemy.

They sat down on a small patch of grass near the rails and waited for their train. It was time they should have spent together, reminiscing, as they would not live together when they got to Sodorrah, but there was too much going through their heads. Everything was new and anything that was old was no longer of interest.

After a few minutes the train came with an ear itching squeal. The sound of the metal on metal brakes and the steel wheels grinding against the track was something that was not heard in their former town.

Patricka was ushered into the second car on the train while Ash tagged along with the other guards to be sure that everyone was sent to the right car. The first car was for those who would be celebrated by the king. The second was for those who would have a professional or personal relationship with him. The third was for the leaders of towns who would be leaving Sodorrah for their own smaller kingdoms in a sense. The fourth through fifteenth cars were for almost everyone else, anyone who would not be dealing with the king on any level other than hearing his decree through the criers. And the last car was for the guards.

Each car filled up with newly appointed callings and one instructor. They were there to give a brief overview of their calling and explain to them what the next steps would be when they arrived in Sodorrah. Many of them would be faced with feasts and parties, some with nothing more than schooling, training, and boarding, and even more would be assigned to a representative of Sodorrah and given not much more than a finger in the right direction.

Ash sat in the final car watching the last couple guards scan the area for any stragglers. He was shocked at the comfort of the train, metal walls, wooden chairs and woven coverings on everything. There were faded oranges and yellows that gave him a slight queasy feeling as he looked out his window.

One of the last two guards boarded the final car, but the other had his arms around a woman and was rushing her up to the front of the train. Her curly hair and tattered dress reminded him of his mother, but he assumed it was nothing more than the homesick feeling he was told accompanied the trip away from your first home.

He watched as the last guard made his way back to the

guard car, hopping up on the stairs just as the whistle blew and the train began its slow but powerful pull away from the transportation depot. Even fifteen cars back he could hear the steam pouring out from the stack in the engine and the amazing strength it displayed in moving such a large payload.

The first movements jerked Ash back and forth a couple times, but quickly fell into a rhythm that was so subtle he did not even notice.

"Welcome newcomers." A guard adorned in gold said grasping everyone's attention with his thick controlled voice. "I would like to congratulate you all on receiving your calling and being so lucky as to commit your lives to the safety of our king!" There was a cheer in the cabin as the new boys felt a rush of importance enter their psyches.

"There will be some surprises and some mind blowing moments as you learn what you need to know to protect our lord, our king, but be assured you are where you are supposed to be and will be among the few whose lives are the most needed in the kingdom." He paused for a cheer that did not come.

"Enjoy the trip. What you need to know before we get there is simple and can be summed up thusly. Pair up with someone who knows what they are doing! Follow them as if you will be lost forever if you lose them, because you just might. You will get your barracks, personal assignment and training after the dinner. Enjoy the trip boys."

Ash moved his gaze from the golden guard to the window. He watched his past world pass him by.

Wyndsoria felt her world fall down around her. Her bed was the only comfort she had left. There was never any connection between her and Moshe, at least not that she felt, but after they acquired their children she finally felt like she did when she was growing up, a part of a family. She even wondered from time to time if the children Moshe chose happened to be her actual birth children. It was always something that was discouraged from thinking, sometimes they even claimed no children from their birth city were available to be chosen, but she felt some kind of connection with her children that was not normal, at least in her eyes.

There was a hole that had opened up within her and nothing could fill it. Her children were gone forever and all that she had left in her life was her hated mission of assuring the water for the town made its way through the pipes laid from the river and her detestable duty of satisfying her husband.

If there was anything she despised more than her calling it was her responsibility to making her husband happy. She would console him and hold him, but there was never anything behind it. There was only the requirement as a wife which she had burned into her mind ever since she was a toddler attending church.

It did not help that Moshe was a priest who always held God's word over her head. She wanted nothing more than to pick her own fate, but as a woman that choice was not her own. She wondered from time to time if the world would have been different if Adam ate the fruit of the tree of knowledge of good and evil. Would women have run the world while men became servants and bore pain monthly?

She shook in her bed. She wanted the thoughts to pass, she did not hold God responsible, it was not his fault that her husband was a man she would rather live without. The shaking did not stop, it ventured from a tremble of disgust to a quake of sorrow. Her heart had been ripped from her.

She thought about what life had left for her and nothing came to mind. She had lost her children and nothing would ever replace them.

Dark thoughts teased her morality as visions of poisonous fruit crept into her mind. The evil considerations were fleeting to the point that she was unsure if she wanted to kill herself or her husband.

She heard a clanking sound of a guard enter her house and she shot up in her bed. Her head swirled as she focused her vision on the room she had confined herself in.

She had no idea the time or why there would be a guard in her house. Maybe she had cried herself through a week and her son was back to greet her. That could not be. No one returned home.

She thought back to her calling and realized she had ignored the water since she went to bed. She probably was being arrested for endangering the town. It was fine. She had no use for freedom anymore.

The clanging of the armor came closer. She heard each step of the guard's boot as he approached her bedroom.

Wyndsoria got to her feet and pulled her robe closed preparing herself for incarceration. She held out her wrists for the cuffs as the door to the room opened slowly.

"Wyndsoria?" The guard questioned with curiosity rather than authority.

"Yes?" She heard the tone of his voice and was taken aback.

"The king has sent for you. Your calling has been altered." He reached out with a small piece of parchment.

She took the paper, trembling from confusion and exhaustion. She could see the kind smile of the guard from underneath his helmet as she slowly unfolded the note.

You, Wyndsoria Wyndhaven, have completed your calling to guard the water source of Listerbourne. You are no longer a Water Bearer. In celebration of your achievement you have been asked by the White King to do him the pleasure of attending a calling completion feast in Sodorrah where you will be given the opportunity to choose from a list of callings that went unfulfilled. Congratulations Wyndsoria.

She looked up at the guard in confusion. She had never heard of someone moving on from a calling before. "The king wants me in Sodorrah?" Tears were invading her eyes.

"For the feast. Yes, ma'am." He averted his eyes and steadied his breathing.

"Will I come back here, to my house and husband?"

"From the feasts I've seen for those who have completed their callings there is usually a choice."

More tears came, now drenching her cheeks, but this time it was accompanied by a huge grin. "You mean I can never come back here? What will I do with my life? Can I stay in Sodorrah? Can I see my children?"

"Ma'am." The guard cleared his throat as he reached a hand out to the emotional woman. "I can't say anything. I just know others have stayed in the capital mansion."

Wyndsoria gave the man a hug. Her arms tingled with the chill of the armor while her chest warmed through the thin robe from the parts of the armor which had been heated by the sun.

She slipped her shoes on and walked out the door.

"Ma'am! Clothes?"

She laughed at her absentmindedness and threw on the first ratty dress she grabbed. She showed no modesty by changing in front of the guard, but her mind was elsewhere. Her mind was focused on the children, hours before, she thought she had lost forever.

Their journey to the depot started immediately as they strode through the town leaving all citizens to question what was happening to her family.

There was no stopping Wyndsoria. She nearly jogged across the desert to reach the depot. Her excitement was unstoppable, making the guard look weak in his attempt to march through the heat and sand.

She knew that it was his armor that held him down, but anytime she had a chance to look better than one of the king's specially trained men, she took it. Of course her living in Listerbourne her entire adult life had given her the advantage of being used to the extreme heat.

With sweat pouring down the young guard's face, making his helmet slip from its correct position, he called out, "You know, they will hold the train for us." It was no use Wyndsoria would not slow.

The trek was long and hard, but she never let her mind leave the thought that her kids were close. She would see them again, she knew it.

When she finally came over the hill to see the train she leapt over the edge falling twenty or more feet just to land thigh deep in the soft scorching sand of the final dune. She struggled to free herself as the guard who escorted her caught up to her.

She ignored the remnants of the buildings, the wires, and even the signs as she made her way to the train. There was no one left getting on, she was late.

She made her way from the last car all the way to the first where another guard helped her aboard. When she got inside the cabin she found herself among one man in rags, two women in stained house clothes and another woman in the most lavish dress she had ever seen. It was four times wider than the small woman wearing it and was adorned with sparkling stones from the hem at her foot all the way to the swooping neckline. Her arms were covered from the shoulder to her first set of knuckles, all with a grayish sheen that matched both her hair and her skin.

This was nothing like the train ride she experienced when she became a Water Bearer. Back then she was crammed into a cabin with hundreds of other teens who were quickly told the basics of securing a water line then stop by stop, practically kicked off the train to fend for themselves.

This time they were given perfume to cover their horrid body odors. They had plates of never before seen gourmet food in front of them and the beautiful woman in the front welcomed them with great appreciation.

"Thank you all for coming." She pursed her lips as she paused. "You have all accomplished your callings and are being rewarded with a celebration the likes none you have seen before." Her silver hair sparkled as she stiffly turned to smile and nod at each of the four people in the car. "There will be great surprises and you will each meet the king as he will offer you choices of how to proceed with your life from here on out."

The woman let out a small forced chuckle as she took her attention away from the passengers and took her seat. Wyndsoria stared into nothingness completely missing the announcement that she would meet the king. Instead she just let her stomach flutter while anticipating seeing her kids again.

After his quiet, reflective walk, Moshe did not notice anything was amiss when he passed by the threshold of the church. His mind was too preoccupied for him to notice the removal of his picture in the entryway. He was too deep in thought to see the new green drapes signifying a first year priest leading that particular parish. It was not until he reached his office atop the stairs when he realized the men just like the ones who had come for his children were in his church to apprehend him as well.

There was no fight, there was none left. The toll of the previous night had drained anything from him that he could wish to have in the current situation.

His blank eyes rose to the gaze of one of the king's men. He let his voice ease out of his throat, "What will happen to Wyndsoria?"

The four men stood at attention while one spoke from beneath his helmet. "As is the law, the White King has sold you to the Fat King. In honor of your former representative and in submission to your new representative, please present your wrists for easy transfer to your new home."

"I understand, but what of Wyndsoria?" Moshe's breathe steadied while his demeanor became static, but ominous.

"The use of the White King's currency is not of your concern, especially when you are pledged to the Fat King." The words came as the men advanced on Moshe. Two of the men had their hands on their swords while the others were ready with the shackles.

The world went dark in the eyes of Moshe as he heard a calming voice reach his ears, "You will live. Do not be scared as I will protect your life as if it was my own. Follow my guidance and your bloodline will reign."

As the first man reached for Moshe's wrists there was a white glow coming from the guard's abdomen. Moshe reacted to the vision with a swift punch to the man's stomach where the armor had an opening for abdominal movement.

No one was prepared for attack. Moshe felt his fist delve into the muscle until it contacted the spine. His hand did not retract, it was held to the body by the engulfing armor. He quickly leaned back pulling the man off balance and whipped him around crashing him into another of the guards.

The next man drew his sword and charged, but Moshe drove his non-anchored foot into the man's shin, bending the armor and breaking the bone. Moshe fell to the ground from the weight of the man whose armor held his hand. The fourth man walked over with a dagger in hand prepared to slice into some part of Moshe's body.

"Submit or I will use severe force!" Moshe could see a smile shimmering in the light from beneath the silver helmet.

He looked up at his captor with one question, "What of Wyndsoria?"

The guard thrust his knife towards the arm of Moshe, but all that could be seen was a white glow that shone from the man's hand to his shoulder. Moshe used his free hand with the momentum of the thrust to bend the guard's elbow moving the blade to his shoulder leaving the armored man's dagger in his own flesh and his hand trapped within the small gap in the joint of the armor.

Moshe lay on top of the two men while the others cowered in pain away from the pile. "What of Wyndsoria?"

The man at the bottom of the pile slid out from the carnage and replied, "She has completed her calling, will be allowed entrance to Sodorrah if she accepts it." He raised his boot to stomp the trapped arm of the priest when Moshe passed out.

The first sight he saw when he came to was the dripping sewage in his holding cell. The air was thick with rot from the sewer and salt from the ocean affirming that he was being held near the seaport.

He had movement in his arm, it had not been broken, but there was an overall throbbing that he could not shake. There was also a sting on the back of his hand from a recent burn mark scarring a mark upon him. He did not remember the punishment he received for resisting, but he remembered what was said of his wife. That was all he had wanted, there would have been no fight if they just would have told him up front. Regardless of how sickened he felt from his own bleak situation at least he knew Wyndsoria was safe. He felt a relief about his wife, but he also knew that it was a passion for his past more than the woman herself.

He let his fingers crawl along the cold stone floor pushing his senses back to reality. He pushed himself up to his elbows to survey the cell. It was full with people who were beaten and battered during their confiscation from their homes. There was no discrimination in the room, all ages were represented within those being readied for the journey.

The moans and dry heaves of the room became discernible to Moshe. The room was nothing more than the full onslaught of the forfeiture of happiness. "Do we know how many are going?" Moshe let his voice crack out past the rawness it developed breathing the murky air.

Nothing but groans replied. Looking at the numbers that surrounded him he realized they must have gathered the majority of those being sold. There was very little space left to house more than those waiting to be transferred.

He looked to his shoulder which had been torn out of his shirt. The purple of his bruised skin mixed with the red of his blood was the last thing he saw until feeding time.

When he awoke again it was to a steel boot kicking his shoulder. The jutting sting created an instinctual cry of agony.

"Eat!" Said a voice from above the spot where he was laying. A steel dish clanged against the stone as the food splattered on Moshe's face from the impact.

He reached over and sunk his fingers into a cold green sludge that was still in scoop form on his plate. As he brought it to his lips he noticed a resemblance the food had to the sewage that dripped down the walls of the cell. Hoping it was the lack of lighting that made the two appear as one in the same, he shoveled the slop into his mouth knowing how much he needed nourishment.

"How long until we leave?" Moshe asked his question through the thick mashed concoction he was trying to get down his throat.

As the food and spittle splattered on the man's armor he looked down at Moshe in complete disgust. "It isn't of your concern."

He reached out with his green covered hand, smearing the thickness on the armor, "I need out of here, when do we leave?"

The man who stood above him raised his foot, but before he could come down on the priest's skull another man shouted from the corner, "Hey! Don't kill him! They don't count until they are on the boat!"

With that the man returned his foot to the floor and took a deep breath as he continued to drop food plates near the sickened prisoners.

As the food hit Moshe's stomach the satiation allowed sleep to return.

The next thing Moshe knew he was being lifted to his feet and set in a line.

The long line of bloodied grey men looked like a line to a battlefield infirmary, but the sight of men leaving the cell to walk out into the light was nothing short of pure hope to those within the walls of the cell. They all knew what was going to happen in the long run, but none of them knew the process.

Although some of the people had done work with imports they only knew what happened once they arrived. A young woman near the back of the line began to prattle off the process for those arriving in the White King's land. "Arrive. Check health. Receive new calling. Receive new home town. Receive sustenance. Go to new home. Pick or receive new spouse." She repeated it nonstop in an attempt to remind herself that once they got to their new home she would be ok.

A man half way through the line fell over motionless onto the wet stone. An injury in his hairline was slowly dripping blood into the sludge on the ground. Two guards jogged over to him and lifted him up.

The first checked for a pulse and then quickly motioned the other to take him to the front of the line. As they went up the stairs to the outside world they could be heard, "Get him to the captain before he stops breathing."

It was a slow torturous wait. Step after step, Moshe was not convinced he could live long enough to see the sun again, but the calm powerful voice returned to him, "Keep calm, you will live through this. You will once again stand tall. Look to your front and your back and see your fellow man. These are my people. This is what is left. Know them, love them, and accept them for they will help you rise."

He pushed through trying to focus on the uplifting ideas behind the voice. Step by step he focused on the inches he moved towards the light.

The painful wait was hardly worth it. Countless men were rushed past him to accommodate their quickening expiration date. The sick smell of the dying and the sewage laden cell crept into his mouth assaulting his taste buds.

After a few hours and few hundred foot walk he reached the front of the line. The sun, now creeping down to the horizon he made it out of the cell before the light of day gave into the long darkness of night.

At the top of the stairs he was confronted by the captain of the ship. He jabbed at Moshe with his index finger and pulled at his skin. He checked his teeth, his groin, his arms and legs. Finally, he was shoved forward with the declaration of, "alive and healthy".

Then he shuffled forward and followed the line that lead to the ship. It was a massive vessel that shimmered in the falling sun. The powerful and dark wood showed no portholes just a towering three hundred foot ship that sat dead still in the port. It held massive sails that could have covered most of his former town.

A man walked along side of those being sold reading off the terms and conditions for their sale. "You have been sold as payment to the Fat King. You are one of three thousand making the journey. Your subjugation to the White King ends once you are on the ship and are then property of the Fat King. Your life, health, and safety, once you are off the White King's land, is in the hands of the captain of this vessel. Any attempt to resist orders will be dealt with as he sees fit."

With that the man jogged back to a later portion of the line where he repeated himself to another group of people.

Moshe stepped foot on the ramp to the boat and looked back at the line. Everyone was walking to what felt like certain doom, but it was for a chance to move on, for the tiny bit of hope that lay within their new home.

Chapter 3

Induction

Sodorrah was the most tremendous city Ash had ever considered existing. It was more than what they taught in school. He had a vision of Sodorrah where there was a mansion atop a hill with many large huts down in the valley. He imagined there being wooden carts set up for a market and a seaport so close the king could use it personally.

The actuality of Sodorrah was more reminiscent of ancient Rome, a humongous working stone city that Ash had no knowledge of. There were paved streets with stone buildings down every one. The markets were housed within humongous open air temples where the wooden carts were set up free from rain. There were wooden huts on the outskirts of the town where people lived. There were businesses set up for nothing more than entertainment. There were play houses, bath houses, an arena for sports battles... There was everything and more that ever entered Ash's mind.

When he first got off the train the first thing he saw was the mansion on the hill. It was a tremendous structure. It had an outer wall that surrounded the entire building, but peeking out above the wall he could see the main part of the palace along with four spires that were each adorned with a flag showing the Penta Diamond.

He stared off into the great white stone behemoth of a castle, forgetting reality when he suddenly realized that it was his destination. The guard he had chosen to latch onto began to walk off towards the mansion and as Ash almost lost himself in his view of the building he almost lost his buddy guard also.

They walked quickly and loudly through the streets. He witnessed people dancing, cleaning, talking, kissing, fighting… It was a whole new world where privacy had a different meaning.

Life in the city was not the life of servitude he knew in Listerbourne. Back at home life was nothing more than doing your duty and having the few moments at the end of the day to spend with family and friends. Sodorrah appeared to be the life that was lived for excitement. Things could be done there that were offensive to God and people's personal morals. It was the worst place a newly free teenager could go.

The sights of the city were awe inspiring, but they did not compare to the approach of the palace. The solid white stone walls housed a door that was at least thirty feet tall that looked to be made of trees the size of mountains.

"Ho! Magisterial guards!" The guard shouted with enthusiasm just moments before the mammoth door slowly swung open.

The vision beyond the threshold left Ash's mouth agape. Marble and stone structures fed into the spires, the ones visible from outside the wall, seemed to rise up into the heavens. They surrounded the palace which presented its face with a large staircase that led up forty steps to an open room where he could enter the home of the king.

He followed his guiding guard to the top of stairs where he could see hallways at the top of more stair cases on the side of the room and a green and white marble dance floor that lie straight ahead, down a small set of steps.

Before he could say anything a guard dressed in a golden suit of armor approached. "Ash?" The golden man did not pause long enough for a response. "Your room is up the stairs to the left. No work today, boy. There is a celebration tonight and you will be needed as a guest. But, remember you work for the king, so any conversation you may have tonight better benefit him."

Ash was left with a strange mix of fright from the threat and excitement from the news. He did not know what to do. He decided to let his mind rest and go see his room.

Patricka's arrival to the city was not the eye opening experience it was for her brother. At her age the immensity of the city was not impressive and the feats of man were nothing more than expected.

She also followed a guard to the palace, but she did not enter the ball room or get boarding within the mansion itself, but instead was sent up to the top floor in one of the four spires. There she was presented with a library that had all the knowledge she would need to begin her duties as an information bearer.

She rummaged through shelves of books expecting to see the same books that she grew up reading in her school. She thought she would find books about the duty of man to God, the history of man's destructive obsession with power, and praise for the white king.

She did not find anything like that. What she found were books that told her a history she had not known. After only looking at one book her entire view of life had changed.

The book she read in the first few hours on the job was called the book of magisterial ledgers. It itemized all the transactions between the five kings.

Each page listed an item being purchased, the cost in human currency, and the kings involved. It was not the basics of the book that shocked her. She knew that the kings used their citizens as their money and that they would barter back and forth. What surprised her were the items being purchased.

The black king purchased an assault on the red king at the cost of one hundred men to the yellow king. The fat king purchased one year's worth of food for him and his magisterial companions for the cost of two hundred men to the black king. Just the day before Patricka received her calling the white king had purchased safety from "the forgotten" at the cost of three thousand men to the fat king.

She did not understand what the forgotten was, but it must have been serious if the white king had spent such a large amount on it. But, the question that kept coming into her mind was why they were buying such things from each other. According to everything she was taught by her priest father, God would provide all those things. Food and security were divine duties and the kings should not have to purchase them. The only things she had previously thought of as purchasable were supplies, buildings, entertainment, and materials.

There was something amiss. She started digging through the bookshelves to see what else she could find when a guard entered the library.

"Miss Patricka?" He stood at perfect attention hiding anything descriptive about him behind his silver armor.

"Yes." The word came out timid and weak, she regrouped and restated. "You are speaking with her."

"There is a celebration in the magisterial ball room. Your attendance is requested."

She wanted to reject and go back to the books, but any party in the palace was most likely being attended by the king himself. She couldn't reject if he had been the one to invite her.

"I will need directions to my room. I have not yet seen it and am in no attire to go to a party."

The guard turned and marched out of the room. Patricka was confused and annoyed, but rushed after the guard not wanting to be blackballed for missing a party.

The boat swayed from side to side causing horrendous pain in many of the people who were being shipped out. Moshe felt healthy as far as the movement of the ship was concerned, but the vomit and retching of the people around him challenged his stomach.

They all stood on the deck waiting for more instruction. The scents of bile that stung their noses were only half as bad as the pain in their eyes from the thick salty air that the ocean blasted in their faces.

The scene was horrific, but there was nothing they could do but endure. After an hour or so on the deck one of the crew stood up on one of the sail supports. He was a short, but powerful looking man. His beard had grayed, but the hair on his head had left him entirely. His skin was one of the darkest grays Moshe had ever seen, the life on the sea had taken a toll on his youthful looks. "Listen up! This is a one way trip to your new home. You want to make it easy, just do what we say and you can continue to wander the deck, eat when you want, and…" The man trailed off as one of the men in the crowd began to scream.

It was not a scream of confusion, but a scream of anger.

Moshe was shoved to the side and nearly crushed as a group of men became entangled in a swarm of fury.

The crew member chuckled to himself and then whistled down to the dock. In just a few moments there were guards shoving their way through the mass of people on the ramp in an attempt at getting some real estate on the deck. They had swords in hand and armor shining in the falling sun.

The surge of violence quelled a bit, but one man did not relent. He charged one of the guards and was met with the hilt of the man's sword smashing into his face. The man crumpled as his motion was stunted by the force of the metal into his skull.

The crew member gave an evil smirk as he announced, "I guess that says it all. Food, then it is off to the beds until we get there. Going to be a long trip in the cabins."

Random groans and swears emerged from the deck, but no one had expected a good trip. Most of them were just hoping to live through it.

The line of people coming up the ramp onto the ship stopped as the cook came out of the stairs from the lower deck. He had a huge vat of some sort of stew in his hands. The people on the deck quieted down and smelled the rich thick scents of the stew, happy to take their nasal focus off the vomit stench.

The cook was used to responses of disgust to his food, but when it was a deck full of prisoners they were happy to eat. He looked up at the short man on the sail support who gave him a thumb down gesture. The cook shook his head knowingly and headed back down to the kitchen.

The man shouted at him as he disappeared into the stairway, "And make it quick we have a whole 'nother cabin to fill after we get these below deck.

When he came back up the stairs he had the same vat of stew, but the smell had soured somehow. It did not matter.

The people waiting to be sold were going to ingest anything that seemed edible.

The cook made his way through the crowd quickly allowing everyone to just dig their hands into the vat and feed themselves like they were children with cake for the first time.

He barely made it all the way across the deck before men began to collapse into a lifeless mush. Those who were still conscious began to panic, but their efforts were futile. Just minutes later they also would fold from their stances.

Moshe laid down on the wood of his own volition in an attempt to avoid later injury. Looking to the sky he tried to pray to God as he lost consciousness.

The ball was an elegant affair. Wyndsoria had been given the pampering of her life. Her hair was cleaned to a soft fluttering feel that she didn't know was possible in adults. A green and white shimmering dress was given to her that matched the decorations in the hall and she had been covered in a white makeup to give her the skin tone of the king.

She was standing in front of the table of honor with the others from the train. They watched a jester perform a show that was obviously not written for them, but for the king who had yet to show up to the party.

Wyndsoria kept looking into the crowds of people who were standing around the floor hoping that her children were there in celebration of their callings. Unfortunately, she could not tell if they were there or not. All the women had such an amazing amount of makeup and all the guards were in full armor.

After more entertainment and multiple speeches about the importance of being steadfast in your calling, the king came out to meet the celebrants. He stopped at each person's place at the table and spoke with them.

When he reached Wyndsoria he reached out his hand to her and she kissed it with as much grace as she could supply. Just the touch of his hand gave her the impression that she was suddenly special. The skin to skin contact with someone as important as him, someone who was not grey gave her a rush of excitement.

He leaned over the table and spoke with quiet security, "Congratulations. You have accomplished what only one in a million can. You have been released from your calling and are free to own your life from here on out. But, after looking at your beauty I would like to ask you to rededicate your life to me." He slowly took in a breath and let his gaze drop from her eyes to her long slender neck to her breasts, tightly bound in the elegance of the dress she wore.

Wyndsoria flushed as she heard the forwardness of the king. She felt trapped and tricked, if it had been anyone else she would have stormed out in disgust, but she could not be so rude to her representative of God. She tried to reply, but the lecherous look she saw in his eyes blocked her voice.

Just as she was about to stand in defiance of her king trumpets blared from all sides of the room. The attendees hushed and all eyes fell to the stairs that led up to the open air landing between the interior and exterior of the building. Even the king broke his sinful glare to watch what would happen next.

The golden guard bellowed an announcement from the center of the dance floor, "In celebration of the achievements today we would like to welcome surprise guests from the celebrants' pasts." As the words echoed throughout the room seven people appeared at the top of the steps.

The trumpets played a slow yet uplifting song as they all walked into the ball room to the beat of the music. It was almost a ceremonial dance that lead them down to the floor.

Wyndsoria let everything she was just feeling from the

king sink away into insignificance. Her children were approaching her, she could tell from the moment the music hit that it was time for her to reunite.

There was no possibility of her smile being washed away, she was in the middle of such elation that she felt she could end her life and live in the afterlife in a shadow of that moment.

Ash was in a magisterial robe that flowed with his every movement. The thick purple wool was supplemented with feathers and jewels that were more valuable than the entire city of Listerbourne. He had a surprised smile on his face that warmed Wyndsoria's heart.

Patricka was dressed to match her mother. Still small from her age she looked like a child trying to imitate their parents.

All three embraced. Patricka sighed. Ash laughed. And, Wyndsoria cried.

All the celebrants were congratulated and spent some time with the people from their past who had been lost after their callings. It was a time for rejoicing and mending of hearts.

After Wyndsoria's initial tears of relief from the few hours she was without her children they began to ask her what is next. She laughed and looked at the table, "I think the king wants me here." She swallowed hard as she attempted to keep her mental state away from where it was just minutes before.

Ash was shocked, almost lost his balance when he heard the words come from his mother's lips. His instinct was to reject it, to send his mother home. He wanted to return her to his father and keep her away from his adult life, but as the words barked in his head he caught the eye of the king who was now half way across the room, but still staring at Wyndsoria.

He remembered the order for all his conversations to benefit the king. It forced a lump to emerge in his throat, but he knew that as an adult he had to do some hard things. He forced a smile, looked his mother in the eye and said, "He is a great man. You can't pass that up."

Wyndsoria looked at her son with perplexity. It was not what she expected when she mentioned the king. She had hoped her kids did not even understand that her insinuation was holding back a disturbing lust that she could not morally disclose to them.

Patricka tugged at her mom's dress to draw her attention. "It might be a good idea. I am learning that things may not be right at home. I don't think we have been told the truth of everything. I am learning things. You may too if you stay, momma." Her voice was an unstoppable force to Wyndsoria. The soft, high pitch of her adolescent daughter was like that of a command from God.

She looked at the building she was sitting in and thought to herself, 'I could do worse. I could be at home with Moshe.'

She nodded as she coughed out some tears. Her enormous smile told her kids not to be worried about her. Ash could feel evil laughing at his attempt to sway his mother while Patricka felt indifference.

They all sat at the table and watched the citizens dance through the night. Eventually Patricka leaning against her mother allowing her hair to be tousled by Wyndsoria's hand asked a question that was nothing more than a homesick admission of change. "What about papa?"

Ash removed himself from the table at the sound of his father's title. Wyndsoria continued to play with her daughter's hair as she watched her son leave from heartbreak. "He has God. His duty to God is not done yet and maybe one day his calling will be complete and he can meet us here." The sentiment was nothing more than an attempt to soothe a worried child, but it verbalized Wyndsoria's fear of having to return to the man that she never loved. As much as she appreciated that he had chosen her to be a part of their family, she wanted to live her own life now.

As the night wore out its welcome everyone retired to their rooms. Ash returned to the guard's barracks and Patricka began her first night in her new home inside the library's attic. Wyndsoria found herself the last guest of the party still inside the ball room. She looked at the ornate decorations hanging from the high ceiling and let the realization of her new life sink in.

The king re-entered the room from a hallway in the corner and walked straight towards Wyndsoria. He wore determination on his face and let his stride seep power. He reached the table where she sat and was pleased to see joy in her eyes.

"I am supposed to wait until morning to present you with the other callings you can assume, but I wanted to present them to you in private. I have a personal stake in one of them and would rather not be humiliated in front of my court." The king spoke the words without malice, but with the shame of a man who knew his position.

Wyndsoria attempted to show her decision without being presumptuous with a simple, "Thank you, lord."

"Then, you have three options that are set for you. You may return to your village be a caretaker for the Children of Choice where you will watch after the children before they have been chosen into a family. You may go to the seaport and feed those who are unfortunate enough to be sent to another land. Or..." He looked into her eyes desperately searching for wantonness for him. "You may choose me as your new god. You can live within my mansion and be a concubine to me. You could live with my other concubines and possibly birth the next king of this land. You will have the life that all people desire with no rules and no boundaries. You will serve only me when I ask and only yourself when I do not ask."

She looked at him after only hearing what she wanted and spoke, "Show me to my bed?"

He gave her his hand and helped her to stand face to face with him. He placed his left hand behind her head and pulled her in for a kiss. His other hand squeezed hers as he led her in the moment of passion.

He pulled back and led her to one of the side hallways. "No, my wonderful. Not tonight. Tonight, you will see my bed."

Wyndsoria was breathless, the king had kissed her and only moments after choosing him over her old life he was going to have her. The world swirled as she followed him down hallways and upstairs. It was an unreal point in time which she could not grasp the reality of.

When they reached the door to his bedroom she took a deep breath and looked at the colorful tone of his skin. She stepped over the threshold while her mind said, 'Ok, I give my life over to him, my new god.'

Chapter 4

New Callings

Ash was introduced to the fact that his mother was a magisterial concubine the next morning as his training began with standing guard over the bedroom of the king. He had trouble sleeping with his moral objection to his own manipulation of his mother the night before. When he realized that she was inside the king's chambers while he was standing guard made him question his own integrity.

Even though three of the four members of his family growing up were within walking distance, it was the words of his father that were helping him through his moment of distress. "We are not to understand the greatness of God. We are not to understand the morals of God. We can only be as good as we can by him with doing what it is he desires of us."

They were the words Moshe spoke when Ash's pet rabbit was injured. The rabbit was suffering and had no chance. They had gone out as father and son to be merciful to the animal. It was the first time Ash had dealt with death and it was by his own hands.

He stood with his back to the door remembering one of the two great moments with his father. He missed him. But, it was God's desire.

He was brought back to reality by a satisfying moan coming from the bedroom and he searched his mind for something else to occupy his time. He thought back to the other moment that he would never forget with his dad.

It was only a few years before. Ash and Moshe were both outside, lying in the desert sand, looking up at the stars of the night sky. It was a peaceful moment that always seemed to ground Ash.

He asked his father how they knew God existed. When they, as grey people, had only the king to rely on how could they know that God was there.

Moshe chuckled hearing his son bring up a conversation that coincided with his work. "Son, only the kings have an audible communication with God, but every once in a while God will try to speak with us also. We cannot speak with him or hear him, but when you ask you can see him."

Ash couldn't remember if what he did next was out of defiance or if it was what felt natural, but he immediately spoke aloud, "God, please show me you are there." Almost instantly one of the stars in the sky began to glow brighter. It increased in size fourfold. Then just as quickly as it glowed it returned to its original size.

It was a moment between God and man. It was a moment between man and son. The two laid there with the satisfaction that God did exist.

Ash smiled at himself. He would always cherish that experience. He clung to it so tightly that he had used it in school. The last paper he wrote before he got his calling was about that moment. It was about his proof of God. Not the star, but his father's assurance.

The door to the bedroom flung open almost toppling

Ash backwards into the new opening across the threshold. The king patted Wyndsoria on the butt and told her he would see her the next day. She walked out of the room in a dark robe, holding her dress from the night before in her hands.

She was escorted away from the room by a small woman that was the same fleshy color as the king. The king himself emerged from the room studying Ash's face.

Ash stood as still as possible afraid that he was not what the king was expecting. His heart pounded as he attempted to control his breathing.

Finally the king began to speak in a soft unsure tone, "You were with Wyndsoria at the celebration last night, right?"

Ash staring straight forward refusing to give his gaze over to the king croaked out a, "Yes."

"Good. Whatever you did or did not say kept her alive. She made the right choice and by proxy, so did you." He gave Ash a couple stiff pats on the cheek and walked past the boy.

Ash let out a sigh of relief when the king was out of view. He peeked around the corner to see into the king's chambers. It was an extravagantly large room with a hanging bed, table and chairs and small spa or tub, Ash was not sure.

He returned to his duty of guarding the room. The words of the king taunted him as he did not understand what he meant. But, three words would not leave him alone, "kept her alive".

Patricka found herself engrossed in history as she pondered the events of the previous night. The odds of three of her four family members being relocated to the same city on the same day were unheard of. She scoured through journals, crier announcements, and ledgers trying to find a similar story.

It seemed as though it was something that happened once every ten to twenty years. There would be a situation where all members of a family except one would end up in the same city. They always settled in the capital city of the kingdom it happened in.

The good news was the people who moved typically became famous and influential people. They were leaders of cities, armies, and churches. Often times they would be adopted into the magisterial family and live alongside the king.

The bad news was that when they did not become famous they ended up dead. And, the missing person from their family always disappeared.

Patricka tried to grasp the idea that no matter how badly she wanted it to happen, her father was not going to show up in the city of Sodorrah. He wouldn't arrive today or tomorrow. He would never set foot there. But, her mind would not allow such a depressing idea. No matter how much logic she tried to force in, her brain always said, 'he will come.'

After going through countless ledger books of purchases between kings, Patricka noticed that something else coincided with these families that remain together. They always arrived in their capital within a week of purchasing safety from the "forgotten".

Even at her young age, she knew there was a connection, but she did not understand it. She could not marry the ideas together.

She looked out the window of the library and realized that the sun was almost to its highest point. She was going to miss her appointment. She had found a letter under her door when she woke up telling her to meet with the white king's naval commander at midday.

She was walking into the meeting blind. She had no clue how to prepare for it, but had decided that she must go regardless.

She set the books down and scampered down the long staircase leaving her library for her appointment. She set out through the open gates and into the town. Attempting to be an adult she walked with a swagger and tilted her nose to the sky. Her tattered dresses were gone and she now wore the wardrobe of a magisterial advisor.

As she made her way through the dirty and sinful city she received countless glares from the drug dealers, prostitutes, and bookies. It was a hated occurrence when a child they could easily corrupt showed signs of working with the king. As much as the rules were non-existent in Sodorrah, it was still off limits to turn anyone involved with the king to a life of depravity.

Her pompous walk with her snoot raised showed that she was not interested in their games which made her someone to avoid.

She reached the bottom of the valley back where the transportation depot was and found a small cigar bar where she was to meet Admiral Devoncote. She wandered in taking a slow perusal of the area. She was unsure how to find the man she was looking for, but was determined not to look out of place doing it.

She did not have to look long as the Admiral found her. The garments she bore were eyesores for the building and were impossible to miss.

"You must be Patricka." He greeted her with a smile and cordial bow.

"Thank you, sir. Yes, I am here to meet you." She felt the idiocy of her statement as it was nothing more than stating of the obvious.

"Please sit. Want a cigar?" He led her to a table in the

corner where their words would not be overheard. He gave her no time to reject his offer as he immediately went into his briefing.

"There is not a lot to report today. The sale went off without a hitch. The payment has departed and the forgotten has gone with it."

Patricka interrupted as she felt the opportunity arise for a question. "What is the forgotten?" She peered over at him with an air of youth, although she intended it to be a mature curiosity.

He slammed his fist on the table. "Why would they bring in a child for this?" The question was rhetorical, his frustrations were unable to be held in. "I can't answer that. No one can answer that. You have to figure it out. And realizing just how much you need to know before we have one of these discussions, I am going to cut this short. Listen to me and remember this word for word. The sale is done. The payment is offshore. The forgotten is with it. The Fat King will deal with it as he always does. No movement on any fronts as all kings are watching to make sure that is taken care of." He immediately rose to his feet and gave Patricka a quick and courteous head nod as he headed back out the door.

She was left humiliated, confused, and angry. How could she do this job? Why did God give her such an impossible task?

She sulked as she got back to her feet to head back to the library.

Moshe awoke with pains all throughout his back. He was lying on a rack of wooden planks. All he could see to his right were more people lying next to him. To his left was the same. The stench of illness overwhelmed him attempting to force him to retch.

The movement of the sea was obvious, the motion made him dizzy, but the vomit and urine stench threw his senses into a whirl. He was unsure how long he had been out, he only knew that after eating the stew he had followed suit with everyone else on the deck.

The room was filled with moaning passengers. Whether or not others were conscious was a mystery. A warm fluid dripped on his shoulder from the bunk above him. Its dark red color let him know that it was blood, but the cold wetness that had seeped in behind his back could have been any of a number of things. He put his hands forward to find how much space he had above him, only about a foot.

His arms on either side constantly bumped into his neighbor, it was as if he was nothing more than cargo. He pushed his hands up above his head and found a wall. Wiggling his toes he found nothing.

He inched his body down towards his feet. Each movement drove splinters into his back and legs, sharp pains made him jolt and stop every few seconds, but his claustrophobia forced him to press on.

After a handful of scoots his feet dangled over a drop off. He shifted more to continue his movement towards the ends of the racks. A large wave hit the ship and room seemed to roll forty-five degrees to the side. His hands clenched between the planks as his knees reached the end of the bed. He stopped with his legs dangling over not knowing how far the drop off was.

Suddenly another passenger heaved and a splattering of bile dropped from bunk to bunk. The internal image he pictured of vomit being dripped down on him reignited his need to get out of the bunk. He kept inching down the wood.

His back numbed from the splintering and his breath became more erratic as the spicy heat from the sickness seeped into his lungs. His butt slipped over the edge of the hard wooden surface causing his back to arch to horrific levels. He twisted his body to ease the pain of the pivot point, slamming his face into the knee of the person next to him.

The stunning impact on his nose forced him to jerk back, lose his balance, and he fell off the bunk and to the steel flooring below. The thud resounded throughout the room receiving multiple startled yelps from others in the cabin.

Moshe had landed on his left shoulder first, followed by both his knees, one on the hard floor, the other on top of that. He throbbed from the impacts, but he was still in one piece. He swiveled over to a sitting position and looked about the room. His bunk was one of many, five up from the floor. Taking in the sight of the dark wooden room he saw ten levels of surfaces. Each plank was about half a foot thick followed by a foot of space. Each level had ten sets of feet visible from his vantage point. He turned to face the opposite way and the same thing on the other side. Two hundred men lie ill and drugged in the cabin. With the stench of waste that was flowing about the entire room it was a wonder anyone was alive.

He sat in the floor and let a few minutes pass unaware of what else he could do when the glowing white light he saw during his fight with the white king's guards returned. It illuminated the soles of the feet that were visible from the bunks. He stood up, shaking from his injuries and exhaustion, and began to tap on the soles of the people's feet. He walked up and down the aisle gently grazing the dirtied skins. As he did, the prisoners one by one began to move showing life re-entering their bodies as the drugs they ingested took a back seat to their consciousness.

Garbled voices shouted out, "Help! I am dying!" The pleas of the souls bunked up like luggage spoke to the heart of Moshe. As they continued, "Where am I? Just let me die!"

he heard another voice resonate above the pain. It was a deep and soothing voice, "Moshe, this is your moment. Suppress all fear and speak my words to your people."

As the next words fell into Moshe's ears he repeated them as he watched the people wiggle their way off their bunks. "This is an insult to your god. As a creation of the Lord you are not meant to be sold as cattle. As a creation of the one true god you are not meant to serve the ideas of five men alone. Over thousands of years the kings have twisted the word of God and destroyed the souls of men. They do not hear the word of the one true God. They do not speak for the Lord. The white king is a messenger to the white people who worships the god of pride. The black king speaks my warnings only to the black people while he follows the words of the god of greed. The yellow and red kings only relay prophecies for the few red and yellow people who walk this Earth. The red king is the embodiment of the god of vanity. The yellow king speaks the prophecies for the god of wrath. And the fat king, he is nothing more than a false prophet."

A few men and children reached the steel floor and were looking at Moshe with awe. "I am Moshe and I speak to God! I will lead you out of hell! I will lead you to freedom and true worship of God! Join me and we will overtake the land of the fat king where we can live in the grey kingdom!"

More and more people were on their feet beginning to crowd the small aisle that separated the walls of bunks. One of the men raised his fist to the air and shouted, "I pledge my life to the rise of Moshe, the grey king!"

A woman looked to the ceiling and screamed, "I never trusted the god of the white king. Hail Moshe, the grey king!"

Most of the shipment had reached the ground with only the dead and dying left on the bunks. The grey mass of people cheered and charged the door. There was no organization, but the collection of people threw all their might against the thick wooden entry point. The metal locks squealed as it bent from the force of the blows.

A man crumbled back to one of the bunks as his ribs gave way to the pressure from the charges. The mob of men did not cease, they continued to thrust against their cage.

Moshe looked to the door and saw the glowing white light shine through the crack created by the human battering ram. He screamed, "Break it open!" and the group charged one last time breaking through the wood.

Salty air came rushing into the room giving the stench of waste a new power. They climbed through the destroyed gate and scattered throughout the lower deck finding more locked doors.

They shouted the words that Moshe had preached through the doors and the ship began to rock, not with movement of the oceans, but from the movement of the people.

The luxuries of being a concubine were beyond anything Wyndsoria could have imagined. After her night with the king she was sent off to a bath. She was disrobed, bathed, massaged, and made back up to look pristine.

She only saw her grey skin for the time between the bath and the reapplication of her makeup. Her hair was silky, her skin was smooth, and she smelled of flowers in a garden. It was hard for her to do anything other than smell herself.

The woman who had escorted her there also was pampered. She was more accustomed to the treatment as when one of the men approached her to wash her, she turned him away with a casual remark, "Not you. I need a more masculine man to touch me." She relaxed in a tub just feet away from Wyndsoria enjoying the rights of a magisterial court member.

It caught Wyndsoria's eye when the woman stepped out of the bath and walked to the massage table. It was not her nakedness, she had come accustomed to seeing people naked when she would enforce water safety in Listerbourne. She was constantly running people out of the river for swimming in the drinking water. It was not a beauty that shocked her as the woman was not attractive.

It was her skin. When she washed she did not rinse into a common grey, but stayed the pinkish white which made the king, the king.

Wyndsoria gaped at the woman until she returned the gaze with a superior smirk. It shamed Wyndsoria and she rested her eyes to the ground for the rest of the cleaning.

It was assumed throughout the kingdom that there were many of the non-grey skinned people as concubines birthed many children for their kings. Some of them were grey and some were not. The girls and boys who did not become king had to live somewhere. It was not a surprise that they existed, but a surprise to finally see one.

Afterwards they were given more luxurious dresses and they left their soiled clothes behind. The woman led Wyndsoria down chamber hallways until they reached a set of golden doors. Here the woman gestured for Wyndsoria to enter and left without a word.

Inside the room was a plethora of sofas, beds, tables, mirrors, and fresh fruits, meats, and cheeses displayed near every sitting area. In the room were three women who were lounging around in robes, each with their own personal bed that could fit a family. They all were barely covered showing off their bodies to the cavernous room.

Each of them was a different shade of white and it looked to be a slumber party of the most pampered women in the kingdom. Wyndsoria feeling out of place sat in the corner by herself and tasted the foods that sat next to her.

Everything was immaculate. She had never eaten food that had such flavors and smells. She had stuffed her mouth with more than it could hold when two of the women approached her.

The sight of them made Wyndsoria shrink in humility. She was caught with a face full of food and an inability to speak without sending food spittle across the room.

The women put Wyndsoria's beauty to shame. They had the defined facial structures that were heralded by the kings, making their jaw and cheeks stand out from the rest of the facial structure. They both had long wavy hair that was colored the brightest of blues and reds, pulled back to reveal their ears and the sides of their long necks.

The first one tilted her head to the side with a kind smile and greeted Wyndsoria, "Welcome to the concubine quarters. I am Genevieve and this is Ruby."

Wyndsoria swallowed her food as quickly as possible, "Wyndsoria."

"You were not born in Sodorrah were you?" Her eyes traced the new girl's body up and down while her mouth twisted in a disapproving expression.

"No, I finished my calling and..."

"I assumed that." Genevieve's tone became sour. "You are obviously an acquisition of a forgotten sale. The king would otherwise never consider touching one as boring as you."

They sat near Wyndsoria, but ignored her. She was offended, but understood. She was a grey posing as royalty, not grey as in the color which they all truly were, but grey as in the peasant.

The other woman came over to Wyndsoria and sat next to her. She was older than Ruby and Genevieve. Her features were sagging and her dress hung a bit different, but she had a kind look to her. She leaned in close and whispered, "Don't mind them. They know you are a threat. They are about to lose a lot of time with the king to you."

Wyndsoria appreciated the remark, but did not understand.

The old woman understood the confused look she received, "We are all concubines and as such we all vie for the king's attention. Those two have all his time right now. Sometimes he goes on three or four day trips with the both of them. But, if you look closely Ruby is starting to show and once he realizes she is pregnant again she will be left here with no affection until she births." There was a sinister smile that accompanied the comment.

"Left here?" Suddenly Wyndsoria feared she would be a prisoner in this room.

"To sleep my dear. We are concubines, we have free roam of the kingdom and as long as our makeup does not run we are treated as if we are royalty. Even when it does people still fear any retribution from wronging us."

"So, you never go out as grey?"

Chuckles turned into a small cough from the woman. "Yes, my dear. We occasionally go out grey. But, if we want to be treated royally then we become white like him."

"This is it? Just the three of you?"

"The king utilizes many girls, but right now we are the only concubines. He does not know which ones will bear the next white king and which ones only birth the useless grey children. Of course I am no longer used. I am here because he can't let me go."

"He never sees you anymore?"

"No, my dear. I am old and can no longer be of use to him, but I am the daughter of a forgotten. I came here when I was thirteen and served him by birthing seven children, all greys. But, since he cannot risk me searching for my father I am allowed to stay here."

The old woman held up a finger as she turned her ear to hear what Genevieve and Ruby were discussing.

"I woke up in the middle of the night and he was speaking in his sleep." Genevieve held out her words for effect, but sounded like a gossipy child. "He was saying that Hubris had turned on him and that he would be chained to his bedroom. He screamed at Hubris for not giving him what he was promised."

Ruby stared at the girl with intense fascination.

"He woke up then. He didn't notice that I was staring at him, but I was. I heard it. It was a dream that I was allowed to hear from the king." She giggled as she finished. "Although any dream that leaves the king chained in his bedroom better involve me as well!"

Ruby snorted with laughter, "You are so right! Thank God for giving us the calling of concubines." They fell into each other's arms in giddy laughter.

The old woman rolled her eyes at the girls and leaned over to Wyndsoria. "Those two are always making lewd comments."

Wyndsoria, unable to comprehend what all was happening asked the woman, "What is a forgotten?"

She put emphasis on her first syllable, "THE forgotten is a grey who speaks to God. Any miracle reported against a person is sent off to the land of the fat king where they are killed."

"Why?" Horror leapt into her voice.

"I'm sorry. Who was the forgotten in your family?"

"My husband did not come to Sodorrah with the rest of us."

"Then it is him. From what I have learned in my years here, the only people who can hear the words of God are the kings, but occasionally a grey hears him as well. The kings do not want anyone encroaching on their duties and snuff out the greys as soon as they are identified. They remove the family from the community and place them close to the king to be sure they do not go after them. There is a prophecy that no grey has ever heard, about the forgotten, and they do everything they can to keep it from coming to pass." She paused and noticed a tear forming in Wyndsoria's eye. "I am sorry my dear." She hugged her.

"No, it is fine. It was just my husband. I did not pick him. He picked me." But the thought of the man who she lived with for all those years still brought emotion to the surface.

The woman held Wyndsoria until the crying passed.

Moshe had an army of grey skinned people and they ran up the stairs to the top deck with an energy unseen before by the crew. The people were angry and motivated, but their actions were not what Moshe had intended.

He was not in front of the charge, he had stayed back trying to help some of the injured get down from their bunks. When he reached the main level everything was a flash of violence. The light of the sun reflecting off the water burned his vision and the goings on were nothing but flashes with a non-stop audio of torture. There were screams of agony, countless splashes into the waters below and sounds of metal slicing flesh. When he could start to open his eyes due to clouds beginning to form, he saw the short man who had barked orders from the sail support being thrown over the edge of the ship. He screamed all the way down until he hit the waters and disappearing into the nothingness of the ocean.

"STOP!" Moshe screamed as the men started to pull a rope against the captain's neck. "They are grey as well!" This message struck the angry mob and they ceased their attack.

They would not let go of the remaining crew. They still held the cook, the captain and a couple of basic crewmen. The men looked up with horror as Moshe walked to the front of the ship.

He stood a few feet from the captain and his two crewmen with his hands behind his back looking like that of a pirate. He closed his eyes and turned his face to the sky.

The voice came to him once again giving him guidance in his time of pressure. "Ask them to follow God, to follow the words you speak for me and if they will not, let my people do with them as they please."

He dropped his head in sadness. His mind reached out to the voice of God, 'I cannot tell these men to kill. It is wrong to murder.' As the words crossed through his brain a bolt of lightning struck from cloud to cloud above their heads. The light of day dissipated and rains poured down from the heavens.

"It is not your morals which apply to my people. It is the morals of God who speaks to you now that affect the decisions made today. Was it immoral for me to free the ancients from Egypt through the plagues? Was it immoral for me to annihilate the giants from the Earth to spread my people across the lands of the globe? It is not for you to say. Now ask them!" The words were so loud, the thunder was almost comforting.

The grey people stood, still apprehending the workers of the ship, waiting for Moshe to speak.

"You have a mutiny upon your ship, captain." The crowd roared with guffaws at the joke from their new leader. "We are tired of the kings of the Earth dictating to us what God has said. We are tired of serving man when it is written that we shall all serve God. We are tired of being treated like livestock good for any transaction. And God himself spoke to me today." He paused as the captain's eyes spread wide open.

He continued, "He told me to lead his people out of the hull of this ship and take them to a land of freedom! We are here to overthrow the fat king and crown myself the grey king of Earth!"

One of the crewmen began to shake with fear. His grey skin trembled from the words he heard coming from his captor. "You are the forgotten!" He screamed as he fought to free his arms.

"I am the grey king!" The ship erupted with cheers. "I ask you once and I hope you will turn to the purpose supplied by God." The entirety of the ship silenced as they waited for Moshe's words. "You, today, have the chance to refute your sinful past and follow the words of the one true God. You can play a role in throwing off our chains of bondage. Say ho, and that you will follow me as we lead our people to freedom!"

The people cheered again, but quickly hushed waiting to hear the reply.

The first crewman said, "I cannot follow the forgotten." He hung his head in defeat. The second said, "You are not God's messenger, only the kings are!"

The crowd began to pull on the crewmen as they rejected Moshe. Then the captain spoke out, "Long live the kings of Earth! The white king! The black king! The red king! The yellow king! And…" He paused as the entire ship turned their rage against the next words to come out of the captain's mouth. "The fat king!"

Moshe dropped his head and turned his back. He listened as the crowd pummeled the men into submission. There was little fight in them. He heard screams of agony coming from the captain as the thudding sound of the crewmen hit the waters. He made his way to the other side of the deck as he heard the slicing of the captain's body with his own blade. The screams subsided as he heard flesh tear under the power of the people.

As Moshe approached the cook with tears in his eyes from witnessing the vengeance of God he heard the applause from the others as the captain was torn to pieces.

The cook looked up at Moshe as if he was the messenger of death. The ominous sea around them left him looking into the eyes of his would be executioner.

"My son, do you reject the sins of your past and turn towards the light? Do you condemn the lives of the men who have enslaved us and taken the world for their own? Do you scorn the kings of Earth and join us in the fight for freedom?"

The cook took no hesitation and screamed, "I do! Long live the grey king!"

The people let him loose with both happiness and annoyance. Their blood thirst going unfulfilled.

Moshe put his hand on the cook's cheek and spoke to him, "Thank you. No one should have died here today. Thank you for seeing the way of God. As a priest from the white kingdom I bless you on this day." He paused as he looked into the fearful eyes of the cook. "I know this is frightening as have been all the great events of history, but just as you were called on to be a cook, I have been called on to be the king."

Chapter 5

Designs

Four days into their new callings and Wyndsoria invited both Ash and Patricka to the magisterial dining hall for a dinner together. Although she had not seen her kids since the ball, it seemed bearable while the few hours after their leaving Listerbourne she thought her life was over.

The three of them gathered around what was considered the peasant table, but it was where they wanted to eat as it was small enough for them to eat near each other. The royal table extended across the room leaving one end out of conversational earshot of the other end.

The conversation was pleasant, but Ash was perturbed by his mother's insistence that he attend. It was out of the realm of normalcy for a guard to go to a family gathering until he reached captain. At that point a guard would start thinking about choosing a wife and children.

But, he realized that since his mother was a concubine she was given special privileges and as such he was given special punishments. He smiled and nodded just as he did when he lived with her in Listerbourne. It felt a shame that he was stuck in the capital city with his mother as opposed to his father. Moshe would have given him the space he needed.

As Ash considered his father Patricka spoke up as if she had read her brother's mind. "Where do you think dad is?"

Ash replied with what the king had hoped he would, "He is back at home preaching to the people. Just because our lives changed doesn't mean his did."

Patricka spun her fork around her corn, "Yeah, I guess so." It was not heartfelt. She knew something had happened. She still hadn't quite put the puzzle pieces together, but she was close, just a few more clues from the books she was reading and she would figure it out.

"Yes, Moshe is back in the village doing the work God chose for him." Wyndsoria smiled at Ash thankful that he had not heard word of the forgotten.

"I don't know. I have a feeling that something may have happened to him." Patricka was trying to be sly, but she felt an obligation to God and the king not actually reveal the findings she had.

Wyndsoria grabbed the girl's hand gave her an affectionate smile. She could see the hurt and confusion on her daughter's face. She had put so much effort into believing that her little girl had become a woman she had not considered if she was actually ready. "He is fine, dear."

She drove the conversation back to the types of things they talked about before Sodorrah, how their day was, what new friends they had… It was a nostalgic look back at what was now gone.

Ash left the dinner as soon as he felt it wasn't offensive and left Wyndsoria and Patricka alone in the dining hall. It was a quiet night where a mother held her daughter, told her everything would be alright and sang her songs.

It was a fair well of sorts and a much needed one. After Patricka had fallen asleep in the arms of her mother

Wyndsoria asked a butler if she could get a bed and some bedding in the room.

With her pull as a magisterial concubine, she was able to spend one last night as a mother helping her daughter move on with her life.

The murky air of the open sea never felt so good. The ideas that Moshe had planted in the minds of the men on board had opened up a hope for a freedom they never knew. The open waters shining with the light of day was the life that lay in front of them. There was no overwhelming feeling of duty to another man just their own fate firmly in their grasp.

The ship only took a few hours before everyone found their job aboard. Those who were doctors before they left acted as the medics of the vessel. Those who were fishermen fashioned poles out of supplies aboard and caught fresh fish daily for the passengers. It quickly went from a prisoner transport to floating city.

After four days at sea the cook started to get anxious about coming into shore. The trip should be about over, but with a new captain and navigator no one was sure if they were even headed to same location.

Moshe had two sermons daily to keep the spirits of the people aboard up. He fashioned his words both around the words of the great book as well as the mission he had been given by God.

He had an audience of a hundred or so as he gave an impromptu midday lesson on the upper deck. "As we all sit under the light of God's life giving creation, the sun, we are reminded that everything has a dependency. It is why he created the sun, to give light to the Earth. Without it there is nothing but darkness. It is why he gave man woman. Without her he is alone and helpless. And it is why he gave us courage. Without it we are nothing but slaves."

He stepped down from the landing he was on and headed down to find the cook. The stairs were dark and cold just as they were when they got there, but walking past the prisoner cabins felt a little bit colder. He would be ecstatic when he was able to get off the boat.

He made his way down the hall and followed the scents of fresh fish and vegetable slop. The two mixing together made a strange sort of repulsion. There was always something that was desired, but the cook seemed to only mix it with something that turned the stomach. Moshe took a hard swallow and considered how lucky they were to open the cook's eyes. He could not have taken another slaughtering on the day they woke up from their stupor.

He wandered into the kitchen to find the cook hunched over a counter.

"You sick? I guess dinner is off for tonight then." Moshe joked with the man as he had become used to seeing people sick. It was mostly from the motion of the sea, but an occasional fight from some of the cook's cooking wasn't unheard of.

The cook looked up with a look of terror. His eyes showed fear that unsettled the newly named grey king. "No. We are close to land. I saw gulls this morning."

The news startled Moshe, but he had been planning for their eventual arrival. "Ok, gather everyone we must make sure everyone knows the plan."

He turned back down the hallway and raced up the stairs. The light of the sun caught him off guard since he had already reacquainted himself with the darkness below. He rushed across the deck to the captains landing where he found the replacement captain and navigator.

He looked at the men with a heavy stare. "Land ho." He almost whispered the words. He could see the impact of the statement as if he just shot a cannonball at the two men.

The lanky, dark haired navigator shook his head in acceptance, "I knew. I just didn't want to admit it. I guess this is it. God help us all."

Moshe smiled at the man, "He is."

The two men dashed off the landing and helped round up as many of the passengers as possible. Within twenty minutes there were a few hundred people on the top deck looking at Moshe standing on the sail support just as the man had the day they boarded.

Again the people looked to the person standing in full view for direction for guidance and for hope, but this time it wouldn't be an instruction of subservience. This time it would be a message of hope and mission.

"The time is upon us. We approach the land of the fat king." The crowd roared with anger. "This is not time to fight. Please put aside your frustrations and show the patience that is lauded by God himself."

The women breathed deep while the men and children countered back, "We did not serve one king to come here with hope and give in and serve another!" Another voice in the crowd shouted, "Death to all who oppose you grey king!"

"If we come off this ship with arms in hand we will see no victory, but our entrance to heaven. We are outnumbered and out armed." He looked out over the faces of his followers searching for approval.

A young woman in the crowd spoke up, "But what are we to do then?"

Moshe looked at the face of the young woman and it was kind and gently, but had the beginnings of a hardened look. Understanding that the young woman probably in her twenties had most likely had her world ripped from her because the white king needed to use her was heart breaking. He could see his daughter's life behind the eyes of the woman. She had been taken from everything she knew and expected to adjust. He did not understand why she stood out. It was just a face in the crowd, but it could be the closest embodiment of the women from his life on the ship.

"We enter the kingdom the way they expect us. We will go back down into the bowels of this ship and lay down on our prison beds. We will be the cargo they expect. Our new captain and navigator will stay up here and bring the ship in."

"But why? How will this set us free?" A small tremble of anger swept through the mob.

"Calm yourselves." He raised a hand and waited for the attention he demanded. "We must build an army. We must do it underground at first, but it will rise up quickly. You get off this ship and process into the kingdom. You receive your new calling and report to your new villages. But you speak of the grey king. You talk about hearing the words of God from my lips! You let every fellow grey know that they are enslaved by greedy men who have taken our God for their own!" Cheers.

"This plan is not mine. Do not applaud me. God gave me this plan last night. He spoke it to me word for word. Praise the father on high. He has told me that others you preach to will see the light and join quickly. In three day's time we take the capital! We begin a new kingdom and set free the grey men of this world!" The roar of the grey mass was abrupt and unsettling. There was a passion in them that could not be smothered.

Moshe hopped off his perch and began to pat people on the shoulder asking them to spread the word so they could be prepared when landfall came. The scene was like that of a knocked over ant hill. Insignificant bugs scattered all about in a desperate attempt to regain any order they had.

He slowly made his way towards the stairs, mentally preparing himself to voluntarily return to the bunks. He looked out for one last glimpse of the ocean. He wanted to have a lasting memory of the world being at his fingertips, but instead he saw the woman who spoke up again.

Her slender grey body was outlined by the wind caught dress that flowed in time with her hair. She was looking out over the waters trying to apprehend her own last sight. Her face was still, showing no emotion. There was too much to deal with for her to be excited.

He did not have to speak to her to know that she felt she had lost everything. The life she had and the desires she had hoped for were all ripped from her for the king's transaction. It was just more fuel for Moshe's mission.

He took a deep breath and turned down the stairs. He felt the warmth of the day hide behind the wood of the ship. He felt the chill of captivity creep back into his reality. It was very real, but he knew it as a necessity to a greater end.

He entered the cabin he had woke up in a few days before. The stench of death and sickness gone, but the memory of it filled his nostrils. He closed his eyes before he climbed up to his bunk and prayed to God, "Please, help us be what we were meant to be. And help us survive this first trial of reliving this hell." He exhaled and climbed up to the bunk he began at.

The words of his prayer echoed in his head as he lie down on the splintery surface he had recently escaped from. Often times Moshe would wonder if he would be granted with his desires if he prayed hard enough or if he asked for the right thing, but this time he knew God had already granted his prayer before he even said it.

As much as Ash wanted to put the meeting with his mother and sister behind him the question that Patricka posed leeched onto his mind. He had no idea what had become of his father. His positive sense of the world wanted to believe that he was still teaching and enjoying his life, but his logic told him something was amiss.

If they would allow their family to be relocated there would have been no reason not to include the patriarch of it. But, with his being left behind Ash got the feeling it was done on purpose.

He tried to go about his duties and serve the king in his role as protector, but he always found himself wondering about Listerbourne. It was a good thing that there were no plots being carried out against the king or Ash may not have caught it. His mind was always elsewhere and his work suffered from it.

His shift was over and he was leaving the palace to go have drinks with some of the other guards. But, he did not head down to the city to partake in his teenaged fun, instead he went to the office of the head guard.

He told himself that he wanted a break from the ribbing of the other guys. Since he had his dinner with his family they all called him mama's boy. Drinks would be nothing more than a continuation of the torment.

He walked along the inside wall of the magisterial compound listening to the soft wispy sounds of the grass as they grazed across his boots. He let his left hand drag along the slick stones that together made the surrounding wall to keep the most dastardly of folks outside the king's private manor. Or maybe it was to keep the king and his most influential of people inside, away from the real world beyond his castle.

Reaching the corner of the wall he stepped up the two small steps into what looked to him like a cottage. He pushed open the thick wooden door, feeling its scars from the years of servitude. The door opened up into a modest room that showed no signs of being the workplace of the most important guard in the country. There was a small oak desk with a stool and a two foot tall cabinet to the side. A more comfortable chair sat on the front side leaving the visitor more at ease than the head guard. There were no decorations, just blank walls.

The only item keeping the room from being a barren, unfeeling cube was the Penta Diamond painted on the floor boards. Ash had never really paid attention to the beauty of its symbolism. The five pointed diamond had the earth at the bottom, its vibrant blues and greens taking a focus on the symbol. It was an image he imagined would have been amazing to see in person.

It had not been since the ancients when a man went outside of the Earth and saw the beauty of its entirety, but the museums housed the ancient photographs of those heathen days. Ever since the elimination of electricity those types of missions were considered out of reach.

Each of the points had the five kings. The white king's face was encased in a white circle. The black king in a black circle, the fat king in a grey circle, the red in a red circle, and the violent yellow king encased in a yellow circle. He wondered about the men. The white king turned out to not look anything like his portrait on the Penta Diamond. He was unsure if it was even supposed to be him. Maybe it was a past white king that was given the honor of being enshrined on the religious symbol.

He had only seen the one depiction of the other four kings and it was probably not even the men who stood on that day across the globe ruling over their peoples.

The world that hung below the men showed that God's creation was always a focus in this life. That he was the ruler over the kings and the kings over the diamond. The diamond represented money which in that day and age was man. People were the currency of the kings and therefore the kings were the rulers of man. By the chain of command God ruled the people through the kings.

It was a powerful image and Ash lost himself in it until the head guard came in the door behind him. "Ho!" He said as he came upon the young boy.

Ash's heart jumped as the man surprised him. He turned quickly to greet the golden clad guard, the color of all the guards in leadership in the kingdom. "Sir, ho." He said as he bowed his head slightly in respect of his commanding officer.

The man motioned for Ash to sit as he came around the other side of the table to the stool. When they both sat, Ash realized that the point of the stool was to allow the golden guard to sit above the other. He was up high, looking down on the visitor like the image of the world eclipsing the size of the Penta Diamond.

"Speak. What is it that brings you to my office?" He put one foot up close to the top of stool creating the image of someone who was poised for attack. Ash recognized the stance and could feel the man was moments away from leaping off the stool to disembowel him.

The intimidation worked and Ash had to visibly compose himself to speak to the man. "I was interested in specialized training."

The leader looked at the boy with a quizzical look. "You are what? A week into your calling? You think it is time to start a course in specialized training?" He rose to his feet and began to walk around the desk to show Ash out. He shook his head the entire time and chuckled as he thought about the request.

"Sir?" Ash took a deep breath preparing to make a quick effort in not being kicked out of the small building. "I know I am not ready for a specialization, but my mother is a concubine."

"What of it?" The guard had no compassion in his voice.

"Her calling means nothing to yours. In fact I am surprised you are even aware of it unless you have guarded her."

"I have sir. Or the magisterial chambers, but that is not why I am asking sir. My mother has taken it upon herself to request my presence for what will be weekly diners. I was required to start my calling a day late as she was being celebrated for completion of her calling and I had to attend." He looked up at the man in gold who had stopped his approach and seemed to be perturbed by the information. "I was hoping that I could start travel training so I could learn my trade without her interrupting."

The guard looked down to the ground and stared at the Penta Diamond deep in thought. He muttered to himself, "Damn concubines getting special treatment. It is as if they think they are the king himself. That white makeup does not keep them from being grey!" He reached into his money pouch hanging from the side of his armor. He pulled out a few coins. "What's your name kid?"

"Ash."

He handed Ash the coins and looked into his eyes as he spoke, "I will try. But, if your mother rejects it there is nothing I can do. It will not be specialization, I could not force you into that before we knew what you excel at. It will just be a short term mission while you get the basics down. Take this and go have a night with the boys off duty."

Ash looked at the money he was handed. The coins were some he had only seen in museums. They were golgoths, the currency the kings used before they began trading populations. He had just been given a gift from the head guard that was worth more than a month's pay.

He thanked the guard more than he should, showing his youth and tendency towards admiration. But, the guard accepted it for what it was and Ash left for the town.

The golden guard smiled remembering his own youth

and trouble-making days as he pulled out some parchment and a quill to write out the request for Ash's mission.

Ash tried his best to walk through the city with dignity, but the excitement of having money, being allowed to run free throughout the town and possibly getting his mother out of his hair was more than he could contain. The walk became a slow jog which eventually became a skip. But, he slowed it as he approached the bar, he would not allow the other guards to see such behavior.

His entrance into the bar was exactly what he had expected. Four other guards saw him enter and they all welcomed him jovially, "Mama's boy!"

He nodded his head in jest but when he slammed his golgoths on the table everyone closed their mouths. The sight of the historic money was not something that appeared in the hands of a freshman guard. The others smiled and laughed, but refused to talk about the coins, they considered the idea that they were stolen and nothing would convince them to become an accomplice.

Ash had changed his ancient monies into the currency of the day and spent it like it was an endless supply. After a couple hours all five boys were staggering drunk and wandering the streets of Sodorrah.

Wanting to spend money Ash told the other boys that he was buying tonight and they headed to the bath house. They clanged as they stumbled through the streets. Many of them had become accustomed to walking the streets in armor, but while the alcohol flowed freely they did not attempt to squelch the sound of their staggering. Their yelling and laughter was heard from half a mile away. They had disregarded their behavior and ignored their representation of the king.

After a bit of time annoying the locals with their loud drunken night, they found a bath house. Once inside Ash walked to the counter and gave the rest of his money to the man behind the desk. He swept it all up and tossed it into a box behind the counter, "Is this for you or for all of you?"

Ash smiled at the spindly man and announced, "That is for me and my friends. One girl each, please."

The man gave the boy a sideways glance as he measured up the guards making a decision of just how dangerous they were. He counted on his fingers while looking at the boys playfully shoving each other in the lobby. "That is fine sir. I will put the rest of your money on a tab for you. Your name?"

"Ash, Magisterial guard." He said shaking his head and feeling the first miniscule signs of sobriety wanting to peek back out.

"Good, sir. Let me get you taken care of then I will get your friends squared away." The man pressed his hand into the small of Ash's back as he led him to another room. Cat calls trailed behind him when the other guards saw him leave with the man.

He was led into a small room that had a couple dozen women lounging around in the nude. It was a sight that rivaled Ash's most intimate dreams. He panned the room looking at the previously forbidden female form.

The women in the room ran the gambit on age and size. From their early teens to their late sixties both nearly skeletal as well as fully rounded, the women ignited an excitement in Ash that was entirely new to him.

The man saw his mouth agape and wanting to move on before the guards destroyed the lobby he suggested Ash choose his companion for the night. Ash wanted to be quick for the man, but he was still going through the girls one by one looking at their faces, frames, and demeanors. He was fighting the arousal as his armor was not forgiving in that manner when he saw his choice.

She was shorter than the rest and bore dark red hair than

came down to nearly cover her light grey breasts. She was not either extreme with her weight. She seemed reserved as she was not socializing with any of the other girls and had not noticed Ash there making his choice.

"I want the red haired girl in the back." His words were firm, but unsure.

"Good choice sir. She is new here. Just two months in Sodorrah, a near virgin at fifteen years of age." The man spoke of the girl like she was thoroughbred. He snapped his fingers. "Ruthie!"

The girl heard her name and presented herself to the men. She brushed her hair back, stood with her chest out and eyes locked to Ash's, just as she had been taught since arriving for her calling.

The man retreated to the lobby to assist the next guard.

Ruthie wrapped her arms around the boy ignoring the shocking cold of the armor and spoke to his still gazing into his eyes, "Do you want to go to the private rooms or the public room?"

Ash drifting in both his fascination with the girl and his intoxication shook his head back to reality, "Public room, got to make sure my boys are ok."

She smiled, but failed to hide her eye roll. She took his hand and led him through a door on the side of the room that led into the public bath. It was a large pool made of stone blocks. The steamy water created a type of haze throughout the room.

There were a handful of men and a single woman each in the pool with their prostitutes for the night. It was a happy scene with a surprising lack of sexual displays. It felt more like a friendly pool party than a room of debauchery.

Ash stood at the edge of the pool peeling off his armor. He looked like a locust shedding its skin rather than a man undressing. He took his attire off one piece at a time while

Ruthie watched from the waters below.

Once he was disrobed he stepped into the stinging hot liquid of the natural spring while still mesmerized by the gorgeous girl who was eyeing him with playful intensity. He finally submerged himself and he was welcomed with a tight and full embrace by the girl who he had chosen.

They played in the water, talked of the fun times they had as children in their respective villages and watched as one by one the other guards entered the room with the girls they had chosen. They laughed as one of the boys chose the oldest women in the bath and another chose the heaviest.

They kept to themselves and connected as if it was a normal date. But, the pressure of the business reminded Ruthie that this was her calling. As the night began to go a bit long she took his hand and an armful of his armor and led him to a private room.

It was a similar set up with a smaller bath, but also had a large plush bed in the corner. The candles that surrounded the room seemed to give off a dimmer glow than those of the other rooms in the building.

She looked at her wrinkled hands and passed up the pool for the bed. She lay on her side with her head propped up on her arm. Licking her lips she raised her eyebrows enticing the boy to get what he came for.

Ash approached the girl, but he felt she was more than just his fun for the night. He lay down behind her cupping his arm around her chest and whispered in her ear, "Tell me more about your life."

She dropped her arm and turned to face him. "You paid." Her tone was reaching for something, but Ash could not understand what.

"You are not to be bought. Tell me more about life."

She spent hours telling him about her life growing up. She spoke of receiving her calling and the transport to

Sodorrah. She told him everything about the past few months working in a bath house and ended up letting out all her anguish while he held her in his arms.

In the morning Ash had dressed from a night of intimacy beyond what he could have purchased while Ruthie watched her knight in shining armor prepare to leave her again.

"I will return." He said sounding more valiant than his age allowed.

"Please, you must! You have been the only light in my life these last few months. I hate it here. The things I have to do. I hate this world for leaving me no choices. I hate the king for bestowing this life on me. And I hate the god who chose it for me." She was rambling trying to find a way to keep the night from ending.

Ash paused as he looked at the girl. Her words should have sentenced her to death. It was against the law to speak ill of the king's actions. It was their duty to appreciate the choices he made and the callings he delivered.

He felt his new found love, of the girl on the bed, devour his duty to his king. He could not turn her in.

He walked over to her and kissed her deeply. She felt his life force radiate through her lips and across her body. He pulled back and said, "I will return. Please, do not say such things again. I am sworn to God and the king, but I cannot be your Judas. Please, hold your tongue and be careful. I will be back soon."

She watched him leave her, both hoping for an end together.

She tapped her foot nervously against the cobblestoned floor. It was the first time she was summoned by the king when he did not want her in his chambers.

She looked out the window of his office staring at the

spire across the lawn. She hoped to see Patricka peering out the window of the library, but she was not so lucky as to get a glimpse of her daughter.

Not knowing the nature of the summons she did not know how to act. Typically she was to be disrobed before the king entered the room, but felt as though it would be disrespectful in his place of work. She instead stood staring out the window pondering the possibilities of the meeting.

Her greatest fear was that he was bored with her. He may be sending her back to Listerbourne or possibly to some other city to fulfill someone else's calling while the king replaces her with someone who was more visually appropriate to be one of his concubines.

She thought about the wise old woman who befriended her and considered the possibility that he was going to execute her to protect the secret of Moshe being the forgotten. If he thought she learned of the mysterious prophecy she would expect an execution.

The idea of her death was not a frightening one to her, but if it meant the death of her children she would fight with everything ounce of her being. The idea dissolved into nothingness as soon as the door to the office creaked open.

The king entered carrying himself with his usual noble walk. He sat down at the desk and asked Wyndsoria to sit as well, across from him.

"I have a concern with one of your children." The words spread panic through her body. "It is unusual for me to bring this up since you no longer have any property rights over them, but since you are mine I wanted to run it by you before I made any decisions."

Wyndsoria flew from her seat to the edge of the desk. With both hands flat against the cold slick wood she ranted in protection of her children. "I don't know what they have done, but they are good kids. Please don't allow anything to happen to them. I know that Patricka is young, so she may be dealing with a learning curve and a maturity issue, but if you allow her to have more time with me she will progress much better. She is only ten and having all the responsibility of an information bearer could…"

The king held up his hand to silence the woman who was sweating out of terror. "It is not Patricka."

She was shocked. She assumed that Ash was old enough to make the transition. He was younger than many, but he had a good head on his shoulders.

The king continued, "The head guard wants to put him on a travel assignment. He has been doing fine, but this will send him away for a couple of weeks. You won't be able to call on him for a while." He looked at the woman with care and worry.

"Oh." She sat back down shaking from her assumptions. "And you are asking me if it is ok to send him away?"

The king grunted at the question. He cocked his head causing his neck to double over just under his chin. "I want my concubine to happy. I am asking how you will feel if that is the decision that I make."

She walked around the edge of the desk filled with an appreciation for the man that she did not know she had. She sat in his lap and let her hand graze his hair. He had genuine concern for her mental state. She ignored his attempt to cover up his request for permission and took the compliment that was hidden within it.

She slowly leaned in and kissed his forehead, "Of course my lord. I am more than satisfied with your company, Ash has his own life to lead."

"Glad to hear. I shall approve the assignment. It should help to have a new guard see the whole of my kingdom anyway." He patted her ass signaling her to rise to her feet and he got up from his chair.

As he made his way to the door he looked down at the handle. He paused with his back to his concubine and told her, "I expect you to be in the concubine's quarters nightly by sundown. But, during the day maybe you should spend some time with Patricka. I'm sure she could use some guidance. Like you said, she has a big learning curve to overcome." He walked out the door.

Chapter 6

Being Held

Waiting for the arrival clerks of the fat king's land come aboard to empty out the bunks felt like a lifetime. As the man from the fat kingdom came in to unload their new citizens the cargo had to lie in wait enduring the horrific existence. There was no issue with the missing cargo that had quietly become the new crew. There was no issue with the cargo silently expecting their chance to de-board. The only issue was with the stench and the wait.

Every time they heard footsteps coming down the hall the loud breaths in the sweat steamed room softened, hoping it was their turn leave. Nearly the last to go was Moshe's room. The men came and pushed open the remnants of the door and began to help people off their bunks. Even after everyone was removed and the cabin scrubbed down, there was still an after-stench of horror.

After the lack of respect for human life set the tone for the boarding of the ship the regard for the health and safety of the cargo when unloading was a pleasant surprise. Each person was gently helped out of their bunk and helped to the top deck. It was a slow process, but one filled with concern.

When Moshe reached the top deck, back into the fresh air, he was assigned a processing agent. They had twenty agents who did a quick health check and explanation of how the rest of the process would go.

It lasted ten minutes before he was back in line waiting to disembark the ship. He stood there looking up at the night sky seeing the stars as he always had. He looked up asking God to show him a sign that the right things had happened since he left home. After looking at the stars for a few moments he saw one of them glow. It strengthened in its shine until it eclipsed any other star in the sky. He smiled at the sign and remembered sharing a similar moment with his son years before. He watched it return to its normal luster and found the motivation to press on.

The boat still bobbed up and down in the harbor leaving those who never got over their sea sickness to have one last bout of illness. The occasional hurl was heard across the deck, but it had become a normal occurrence over the trip. The passengers didn't think much of it anymore.

He was unsure what exactly was ahead of him, but there was a feeling he could not shake. Whatever was ahead he did not believe it to be easy sailing. He knew that God had been protecting him and expected it to continue, but even that was not much solace to the hard times he was predicting.

The line moved slowly, but he made his way down the ramp and to a woman who sat at a table. She was skinny. Far more slender than anyone he had known in the white king's kingdom. Her skull was clearly visible as were the bones in her arms.

The people in front of him told her their names and they were given a calling written on a piece of paper then directed to which form of transportation to take to their new homes. Some of the people were happy and excited, while others were still shaken from the events of the last week.

Moshe reached the table and was asked for his name.

"Moshe" He said with no emotion.

The woman looked through her book and paused when she found his name. She looked up at him squinting her eyes slightly as if she didn't believe he was real. Her eyes dropped to the burn mark on his hand from his initial abduction and nodded her head slowly. She placed both hands flat on the table and said, "You will need to go to the palace for your calling. Please go with the guards to my left." She breathed at purposefully steady pace trying to hide any fear she had.

Moshe nodded to the woman and walked over to the guards. Two of the guards nodded to each other and led Moshe to a horse drawn carriage with their swords drawn, walking on either side of him.

As he climbed into the fully enclosed carriage some of the people in line began to ask where he was heading. Slight alarm resounded about the other passengers, but the plan held tight. They did not respond with violence or action of any type.

Moshe sat in the carriage and one of the guards climbed in with him. They sat across from each other, face to face in the dark box. Although little was visible from the dim light provided by the moon, Moshe could see the malnutrition that was evident in the guard.

He was adorned with the same style of armor as the guards from the white kingdom, but it did not hug his body as it always had where Moshe came from. There were gaps in the uniform in the stomach and on the upper legs. There just was not enough meat on the man to fill out his armor.

They did not wait long before the driver snapped the reigns and they were off. The wooden wheels clacked relentlessly against the rocks and sticks on the trail. There was no apparent road. There was no pavement or organization, just open land where they headed off to nowhere.

Moshe had only a small barred window to look out and he saw nothing but darkness. He leaned back in his wooden bench and struck up conversation, "Where are we headed?"

The guard cleared his throat and responded very matter of fact, "The capital city of Myhrrmur." He continued to stare straight forward showing no emotion from the lower half of his face peeking out from the helmet.

"Can I ask why I am being taken away while everyone else gets their callings?"

"No."

Moshe sighed and watched the new land pass him by.

Wyndsoria took the king's advice and spent the next day in the library with her daughter. She had hoped for a loving day where they could reminisce about the happiness of their family days, but it turned into a day of work and study.

Patricka could not afford to spend a lot of time talking and remembering the past when she had to learn to find the information she needed before she had another meeting with the admiral.

Through hours of perusing books they both learned that it had been five hundred years since there had been a real invasion attempt. There had been recent attempts of one king invading a single city, but it appeared that the other kings would step in and quell the problems before anyone could truly seize any land.

Five hundred years earlier the yellow king attempted a true overtaking of the red kingdom. He had paid off the other kings not to intervene and then had built an army in secret to invade the land of the red king.

The attack was led in the middle of the night where ten

thousand grey men landed in the seaport and laid siege on the capital city. It was unsuccessful in the end when the grey servants of the yellow king could not manage to eradicate all the red people. At the time there were approximately forty red people living in the kingdom and only five survived the attack. The king was assassinated, but another male was brought up to take the throne.

The story was shocking to Patricka as she always heard about the kings asking for protection from God. It was assumed that it was what kept wars from breaking out, but it appeared that over the last five hundred years there was no point in it.

They learned a lot about the ancients who used the abominable technologies that modern man was protected against. They nearly killed off the entire species when God forced them into a war where weapons that could disintegrate entire islands were used on nearly every spot of the globe.

But, no matter how many books Patricka went through she never found anything about the forgotten. She did not want to attend another meeting without that bit of information.

She threw her book across the room filling the long silence with a loud bang as the book hit a shelf. She growled with frustration and put her face into her hands.

Wyndsoria looked at her daughter with a desire to fix all her problems. She walked over to her and put her arms around the girl.

Patricka pulled away from her mother, "No! Mom, that isn't going to help. I can't be your helpless daughter anymore. I have to be an adult and learn everything in this room."

The woman felt horrible for her daughter, too much had been forced upon her. She could not run outside and play games with other kids but, instead she was stuck in a lifeless room attempting to learn more than anyone else her age should be forced to.

"Why isn't it in here? I have gone through hundreds of books on our history and the current world and nothing!" She slammed her fists down on the arms of the chair she was sitting in. "What is the forgotten?"

Wyndsoria breathed deeply taking in the dusty paper smell of the room they were in. She looked her daughter and sat back down in her chair. "Honey, I know a little bit about the forgotten." Saying the words was like a spear into her side knowing that the more Patricka knew about the subject the more likely it would be that she would figure out that her father was most likely dead.

Patricka looked up from her aggravation. "You knew and hadn't said anything!" She was appalled by her mother's lack of transparency.

"You never mentioned it! And, I don't think it is a good thing to be talking about. What I have heard is something that shouldn't be shared."   She was already regretting mentioning it.

Patricka crossed her legs and looked to her mother as if she was about to be read a story. Her hands folded in her lap and her face was painted with the look of an inquisitive child.

"What I have heard is that the forgotten is a grey skinned person who can speak with God." She left her statement simple, not too much information.

Patricka let the words tumble through her head. They danced with her previous knowledge of God and realized that she had never heard of anyone of grey skin communicating with God. She had been drilled with the idea that only the kings could do that.

She considered what it meant that her father was traded during a protection from the forgotten sale when something dawned on her, "Do you think dad could speak to God?" Her eyes were wide with fascination and new respect for her father.

Wyndsoria did not like the conversation. She did not know what Patricka knew, but she wanted her to not think about her father who was most likely dead in a field. "I don't know why you would think that." She paused, but as she saw Patricka open her mouth to respond she added, "And, you need to keep reading." The stern tone still had its desired effect on the girl. She returned to reading.

Patricka did use the information though. She went over to a shelf she had yet to pull any books from and picked a stack of the oldest books on it.

Wyndsoria looked up and saw her daughter pulling books off a shelf labeled religion and immediately became curious. She joined her daughter and grabbed some for herself.

Sitting back in their chairs they opened old dusty books. They added small particles to the air that reflected in the sunlight coming through the slats in the shutters. They opened some of the books prepared for a long few hours of reading.

Unknown to them, the books they were reading were some of the rarest information in the world. They were one, of the only handful, of copies left from the religious texts that hundreds of years prior had been removed from the offices of the priests. The texts were now banned from the religious teachings of the church.

Ash finished up his guarding duties in front of the king's chambers just after sunset. He had become accustomed to the humiliation that was his mother having a personal relationship with the king.

But, as he made his way from the hallway in front of the king's chambers he was happy. He had a purpose. He was going back to town to see Ruthie. He had never wanted to see someone so much. The elation he felt just from the thought of her was beyond any gratification he had ever experienced.

He quickly walked down the hall, the coins from his first payday in his pocket, when he turned down the stairs when he nearly collided with the head guard. He bowed his head in respect, "Sorry."

The leader smiled at the manners of the young man, "No worries. I have good news."

Ash stood at attention waiting for his news.

The golden guard continued, "Your request for travel has been approved. I couldn't get you out for very long as you are not ready for specialization, but your mother will be out of your hair for two weeks." The man smiled at the shocked look from the young guard. "Report tomorrow, at sunset, at the transport depot." He turned and walked away content with his ability to help a young promising guard.

Ash was shocked, but it was because Ruthie had driven the plans for travel away from his thoughts. He had wanted to get away from his mother, but this would get him away from Ruthie also.

He decided he had no time to waste. He sprinted out of the palace and through the gates. His mind was determined to speak to Ruthie before he had time to jump to conclusions.

The sights of the city were wearing on Ash. He no longer noticed the smells of the foods or the decadence of the people. He was just another person in the town of no morals.

He jogged down the hill, past the bar and around a corner that led him to the bath house. He slowed his pace as he crossed the threshold.

He was bent over panting from his run when the spindly man noticed Ash's return. "Welcome back." He came over from behind the counter with a very enthusiastic handshake. "Please, have a seat. I can take you in to pick again today, but catch your breath first."

Ash fell to a knee in exhaustion. He looked up at the man, "Thank you, but no need. I want to see Ruthie."

The man let out a tiny laugh as he went to get Ash some water, "I see. You were addicted after one night. I must say, that happens often, but why don't try another and see if you might enjoy a different flavor?"

"No. Ruthie."

The man was disappointed in the response, but was not going to refuse business. He went into the choosing room to fetch the girl.

Ash had been able to slow his breathing and get to his feet just in time to see Ruthie come through the door with the spindly man. She had a worried look on her face when she appeared, but once she saw Ash her face lit up with glee. She walked over to him trying her best to follow her training while she was in front of the workers of the bath house, but she couldn't fight her happiness.

She reached him with a hug that lifted her off the ground. The metal from Ash's armor caused goose bumps to sprout across her naked body, but she did not react as she was happier than she ever had been.

Ash looked her in the eyes, "Go get dressed, I want to take you to my place."

She shook her head as her eyebrows raised to try to speak to him. But it was unnecessary, the small man offered his own words to Ash, "I'm sorry sir, but the girls are not allowed to leave the bath house."

Ash tilted his head and thrust out his chest. "And being a part of the magisterial guards will not curry any favor in this establishment?" He paused as he thought. "I'm sure you have an inspection coming up." He felt the remorse as soon as the words left his lips.

"Oh." The man narrowed his eyes at the boy. "Of course."

"I will gladly pay double the fee for the night." He was desperate to quell his guilt for threatening the business.

The man perked up a bit when he heard double the fee and smiled at the guard. "Very generous of you sir. Please, go."

Ash looked down at Ruthie with teeth grinning. "Come on, get dressed."

She looked up blushing and ashamed. "We are forbidden clothes here."

Ash looked at the man behind the counter wanting a robe or something, but he was ignoring Ash to keep from anymore forced rule breakings.

Ash threw caution to the wind and grabbed Ruthie's hand. They were out the door and running towards the palace. It was the second time in two days that he had broken the law for her. As lax as the city was, it was not permitted to be nude in the streets, much less encouraged by a guard.

They rushed up the hill towards the palace. He moved quickly as his training was starting to pay off, but she lagged behind as she was not accustomed to running. She kept seeing people staring at them out of the corners of her eye. She could take the embarrassment, it paled in comparison to her calling. The cat calls and lustful stares were nothing new to her.

They reached the gates to the mansion and they dashed through, up the steps and then the stairs. When they were inside the mansion, the reaction was different. A couple women gasped while most of the men averted their eyes. The only person who took a serious interest was the king. He had been down in the ball room. He looked up to see a naked girl in his mansion who he did not know. He took note of who it was that was dragging her. He always remembered details for when they might come in handy.

They reached the guard's barracks and flew inside, slamming the door shut behind them. Ash, panting, asked, "Do you think anyone saw?"

Ruthie broke out in uncontrollable laughter as she was wondering if anyone didn't see her. They sat on the floor leaning against the door enjoying the humor.

The night was magical. They spent hours just discovering each other's bodies and connecting in a way neither of them thought was possible.

Ash felt that he had found the person he was meant to be with and Ruthie felt a compassion that had been absent from her life since she arrived in Sodorrah.

They enjoyed each other's passion and eventually laid in the bed looking out the shutters at the stars. It was a beautiful moment. Ash smiled as he rejoiced in the fact that he held the world's most gorgeous woman in his arms and was looking at the stars that he envisioned his father also seeing at the exact moment.

He watched as one of the star near the horizon glow brightly and he knew his father was seeing them also. He kissed the girl's head, smelling the sweet scent of her hair.

He sat up abruptly and put his hands on her thighs. "I am choosing you when I get back."

She looked at him puzzled, "When you get back from where? Choosing me for what?"

"I have to travel for a couple weeks. It is part of my training in seeing all the lands under our king. But, when I get back I am choosing you for my wife." His heart sank when her expression darkened.

"It is part of my calling that I can't marry." She looked down at his grey hands upon her lighter thighs. "I was not supposed to leave the bath house at all."

Ash let his mind scurry through itself as he tried to find a solution. "I will find a way."

She leaned in and kissed him softly. "No, it is not possible. You have already made my life better."

He let her lean on him while he ran his fingers gently across her skin. He would find a way, he was determined.

In the morning he gave her one of his robes and they walked back to the bath house. He had collected all the money he had and brought it with him as he returned her.

When they arrived he told her to keep his robe for the next time and she went back into the choosing room. He watched her disappear and went to the man at the counter. "Here." He put his entire fortune on the counter. "With what I still have in my account how many nights will that buy with Ruthie?"

The man smiled a smile that was only appropriate for a weasel as he counted the coins and slid them into the drawer. "If she stays here, this will buy you twenty nights. If you want to gallivant her around town as inappropriately as you did last night, then ten, if that."

He slammed his palm down on the counter in victory. "Good. Then for twenty nights she is reserved for me. If I show up or not, she is reserved. I don't want anyone else touching her."

The man smiled and nodded his head more interested in the money than the conversation.

Ash brought his finger into the man's face, "No one touches her for twenty days." His tone was serious and steady.

"You paid my good man, I got it."

After a long journey in the cab of the carriage they arrived at the castle. It was a humongous structure with bulbous spires at the top of each wing. They were adorned in amazingly vibrant reds, blues, greens, and golds.

He was led into a side entrance with nothing more than an old maple door that had been reinforced with steel to hold it together. Inside they walked down numerous dark tunnels lit by hanging torches which had left soot marks all across the ceilings.

After a few minutes of walking they came into a small room with high ceilings. It also had the soot marks with four burning torches. The room appeared to be the throne room as the king sat in a golden chair that was formed to support his enormous weight. The small armrests acted as tables for his fat that was oozing off his frame.

There was a table filled with foods of all sorts just within arm's reach of the king. It looked as though half the food had been devoured and the far end of the table was filled with bones and grit with some of it fallen to the floor leaving a scatter of trash.

The fat king looked at Moshe chomping away at some unknown food. His face was lost in the blob of man that sprouted from the top of his shoulders. He began to talk with a deep almost garbled speech, food spittle flying out of his mouth, "So, you are Moshe." He wiped his mouth with his massive grey arm, breathing heavily from the stress of movement. "You are the third forgotten sent to me since I have reigned over this kingdom. I know that you do not understand what is happening. But, I think it is only fair to explain to you the circumstances of your death."

Moshe took a step towards the throne, but he was met with two swords set inches from his throat.

"There are four men in this world who have the authority to speak to God, the white, black, red, and yellow kings. The kings of one color, as I call them, have been given the calling of speaking for him. But, occasionally there is another. A grey skinned man who shows signs of being God's mouthpiece. This man is a threat and must be squelched."

Moshe looked at the king with swords blocking his view, "But, sire, you are grey and you speak to God. You are a king as well."

The disgusting sack of a man laughed with such deepness Moshe could feel it in his chest. "I have never heard God's voice. If I had I would not be here. You were a priest, but you never heard the forbidden scriptures, did you? Five men will speak the words of God. Four men will rule the Earth. The fifth will not die at the hands of men for he will have God's light with him. Any man who attempts to slay him will be slain. This is you for this generation."

Moshe took in the words, but felt like he was being fed a fairy tale. He had never heard of forbidden scripture and was not about to change his beliefs based on the stories of a slug of a man who was about to kill him.

"Understand that I will not kill you. But, you will die. This is how I remain a king. This is how a grey skinned man accomplishes the greatest feat possible in our world. This is how a man like me becomes a king. This is how I become the common king of the scriptures. I take care of the forgotten, the fifth man of the forbidden scripture, for the kings of one color." He looked at the guards and told them to take him to the dungeon.

Moshe instinctively went on the offensive and he had two swords again inches from him. Then he heard the voice of God, "Go, this is your mission, I will bring you nourishment. Do not fight today." So, he went.

Chapter 7

Exiled

Back on the ship when Moshe had laid the plan out for the passengers, he had not realized why he said they would take the capital in three days, but those were the words that God had given him to say. Now, sitting on cold stone in the bowels of the fat king's palace, he knew he only had to last three days.

It had been less than twenty-four hours and the hunger and thirst were becoming unbearable. Inside, the dark damp dungeon reminded him of the holding cell he was in before leaving the white kingdom. The difference was the lack of windows which removed his ability to judge the passage of time.

Every minute created a new growl of pain in his stomach. He paced around his small cell to keep from going mad, but the hunger would hit and double him over in agony.

He looked about the dark room which was lit with a single torch overhead and wondered if it had been built just for the forgotten. Generation after generation of people in his position sat in that room and went crazy. They suffered on that very floor until death rescued them. This was the fate of men who heard the voice of God, but Moshe would not allow that fate. God had chosen him and he would not squander the honor.

He imagined the great men who must have withered away under that ceiling. The men who must have spoken to God, but for some reason did not find the protection from him that should have come with it.

A thought struck him. The kings are from a bloodline lineage. The kings conceive children with their concubines until they find a son born of the right color. That son becomes the next king, one of the only men who can speak to God himself. But, what about the grey men who can speak to God? Are they all from a single bloodline?

Was it possible that the last man to die alone in that prison was Moshe's birth father? Could the men who are found and rounded up be from a single line of people who are only hard to find because of their modern culture's habit of giving children to the community?

The thought was a lot to take in and it boiled a hatred for the kings in Moshe's core. The intensity of the anger was not good for him while he needed to survive. Instead, he went to the corner and folded up in fatigue.

Patricka walked down the streets of Sodorrah with her mother. It was her second meeting with Admiral Devoncote and she felt prepared. Wyndsoria went along for the trip just to have something to do. She was tired of being cooped up in the library and the concubine's quarters.

They passed all the sights and smells that made the town what it was. Patricka kept her gaze straight ahead, she did not want to clue her mother in to her interest in anything that the town had to offer. They glided away from the palace and through the dirt of the people, both walking with their most royal of gaits.

No one offered them anything, they just went about their daily business as if they did not exist. There was no point in trying to influence two women who were a part of the magisterial court, the only thing that could possibly come of it was punishment from the king for doing something so idiotic and harmful to his wishes.

They passed the bars, the bath houses, the markets, and the playhouses. On this day Patricka would be meeting the admiral at the battle stadium. It was a replica of an arena built before the ancient heathens. It was a circular open air building with rows of seats all the way around.

The originals were built for both gladiator fights as well as equestrian events, but the modern day recreation was for battle sports. The sport was a fight to the crippling where teams would disfigure each other scoring points for each body part they disabled on the opposing team. The winner was the team with the most points when time expired. The only exception was in the case of death. Death was not allowed in the sporting world and removed half the points of the team that committed the murder.

Wyndsoria hugged her little girl goodbye and let her go into the stadium alone. She wanted to be there for her, but she had to do things alone now. She was an adult of sorts and Wyndsoria recognized it.

Patricka walked through the stone archways to the seating area. It was a huge structure that made her feel as though she was completely insignificant to the world. The sounds of the crowd resonated around her while a sensation of falling forward towards the battle grounds overwhelmed her.

She walked along the stone pathway looking for the man she had seen at the cigar bar just a few days before. The amount of people made it an impossible task when she realized they would have to be able to hear each other. She headed for the luxury boxes at the end of the oval seating. She passed people doing everything she could imagine. There were fights in the stands as well as families having lunch. She passed two people who were kissing with such a passion that some of their clothes had been partially removed.

She worried, as she saw everything, about being an adult. It seemed as though there was no structure to how an adult was supposed to act. The world felt safe and protected as a child, but now living as a grownup she felt the chaos.

Walking around the bend she came to the luxury boxes which were distinctly different from the rest of the arena. It was painfully obvious that this portion was not as historically accurate as the rest. The walkway led into a dark hallway that had stairs going up and down. Each staircase had stone doors on either side every fifty feet or so leading into one of the boxes. She looked down the stairs towards the playing field then up towards the top deck which is where she saw Admiral Devoncote leaning against a wall smoking a cigar.

He nodded to her and showed her into the luxury box. It was a large room with all stone furniture. The extravagant foods that she had come to expect, in dealing with the important people of the kingdom, was there and laid out perfectly.

They sat down in the armchair stones and looked out over the field. The teams were coming out to begin the battle. The roar of the crowd was apparent, but not distracting. Devoncote gave her a sideways glance and began his briefing, "The forgotten should have arrived. We are waiting on our intelligence to confirm the arrival and disposal."

Patricka took notes and casually responded, "What is the disposal method? I don't want to report to the king that there has been a massacre because someone tried to kill him by hand." She wanted to smile so bright that it hurt the admiral's eyes, but she held back. Her accomplishment of finding the forbidden prophecy would have to be enough for her.

A smile arose from the apprehension of the admiral. "You did your homework. No, disposal should be by his own hand, but that will be in my next report."

A cheer came from the stadium as one of the members of the blue team had his hand severed. Patricka noticed the gore, but pressed on, "What about the fat king's military? Any movement?"

"No. He has been solid for quite some time. He isn't normally a problem for us." He turned back to the game as a red team member had a spear thrust through his thigh. "There was an explosion at a teaching seminar in the yellow kingdom. We think they may be looking for a transaction to acquire replacement teachers. It might be a good idea to mention that to the king as a possible leverage point for a trade, but at the same time it could result in the black king supplying in trade for an attack on us."

Patricka scoured her mind from the hundreds of books she had read to make sense of this. "In response for our damning of the river?"

"Correct, it was their major water supply, but the king wanted it dammed up to ensure a full harvest that year." There was another cheer from more bloodshed. "There is no movement yet from any armies. I believe there will no further information from any possible threats until the forgotten has been eliminated. It puts them all on edge."

"Thank you for your time." Patricka stood and headed to the door excited about how well the meeting went.

"You might want to wait." The warning from Devoncote was not heard as she was out the door before he could catch her.

Wandering back through the stands was a little more

difficult. The fans had become rabid from the violence. There was little room to walk in the pathways while brawls were breaking out every which way.

She was shoved back as two women leapt out into the walkway. They were screaming at one another, pulling hair and scratching the skin of the other away. A man on the field had his leg broken by a hammer just as one of the women slammed her face into the stone railing.

Patricka tried to turn back, but there was another fight behind her. It was five men boxing with all their force. There was no telling who was aligned with whom. The fans had fully invested in their teams ready to go one on one with anyone who opposed them.

The two fights were closing in on Patricka's position. The women were quickly clawing their way towards her with wide eyed, bloody terror in their screams. She tried to hop the rail to avoid the clash, but she was bumped and tumbled down into the seats. She hit seven rows before she collapsed into one of the concrete benches and lost consciousness.

The room seemed to continue to get smaller. The single torch at the top of the room made everything a little bit smoky and almost too hot to bear. He felt every drip of perspiration. He thought he was losing his ability to breathe through the smoke of the torch.

His mind was losing grasp of reality when the door opened. He swiveled his head towards it, "Who's there?" The words came out deep and hoarse as his throat was too dry to allow for normal speech.

Through the light of the door he saw the girl from the ship that had caught his attention on the day they returned to the bowels of the ship. She looked out the door before she closed it behind her.

"Have we taken the capital?" Moshe was hopeful that he had survived his imprisonment.

"No, my lord. I am here to give you some water." The girl said as she pulled a large sopping sponge out of her deep pocketed dress.

He reached out for the sustenance and pressed it to his burning cracked lips. The water slowly trickled from the sponge causing him to cough and spew from inhaling the water. His throat was dry to the point that the lubrication needed to swallow was not there.

He tried again and got a little down feeling the cold travel all the way to his stomach he felt that he was a little more alive than a few seconds before.

"My lord" The girl started, "I will try to bring you more later."

Moshe reached his hand out to her shoulder. "Thank you. How long have I been in here?"

"It has been just over a day." She looked into his eyes revealing her desperate need to get out of the room.

"But, how did you get in here?"

"I was given the calling of cleaning the castle. I have all the dungeon keys. Once I found you I had to help. I can't bear to see my king this way." She was shaking and repeatedly looking at the door.

"Go. Thank you. Be safe."

She smiled and retreated to the door. He watched her as she went and brought the sponge back to his face. The water was life giving to his body. His mind recovered some and things such as breathing were no longer exhausting. He looked at the ceiling and thanked God for sending her.

Ash had spent hours riding trains and horses, but he had finally reached their first destination. It was the city of

Dwellnish which was well known throughout the kingdom for its food crops.

There was a lot of expectation for what the city would look like. Ash envisioned it to be nothing, but lush gardens replacing the streets with bakeries, butchers, and markets everywhere one could look.

He sat on his horse at the gates of the city. He was being led through the kingdom by Jaso a senior guard whose specialty was travel security. He was a quiet man, but kept Ash informed on why they were doing each step of the process.

He learned that they rode horses to all the cities because roads were not always available. They brought water and food with them because not all cities were welcoming to guards. They even carried concealed weapons in addition to their visible ones in case someone tried to surprise them by swiping their swords.

But, the lessons were over for now, they were about to make their rounds through the city and search for anything out of place. The city of Dwellnish looked more like a fort with its large wooden fence. It was just outside a river that housed many predators which would destroy their export to the king, food.

They led their horses to the gate and Jaso kicked the wooden door while shouting, "Ho, magisterial guards!"

There was a lot of commotion behind the gate before the door quickly swung open. As the vision became clear, Ash felt his expectations fizzle away as he gazed upon the normalcy that lay inside the walls of the city. There were no gardens that lined the streets, no water system to keep everything lush, and not even a baker, butcher, or market in sight from the entrance.

They trotted their horses with all the eyes of the city trained on them. Ash could feel the hatred and blame emanating from the psyche's that surrounded him. It was the first time he felt the blame of someone else cast on him.

Jaso was unfazed by the associated responsibility from being a guard and kept his horse moving at a leisurely pace. They paced slowly until they reached the center of the town. The wooden shacks around the dirt road were the main visual of the town. A few businesses had signs to display their specialties, but for the most part it was nothing but blank buildings existing in a nothing city.

Jaso dismounted and tied up his horse as he walked into the only bar in the city. Ash followed closely with his hand on the hilt of his sword. Entering the bar they again could feel the discomfort of the citizens. The music that was apparent as they slid the doors open ceased with their first steps onto the creaky floor planks.

They barkeep looked at the two and quickly scanned the rest of the room. "How long you staying?" There was venom in the voice.

"Two beers." Jaso pulled a few coins out of his coin purse.

"Put your money away." The man bent down to retrieve the glasses for the beer. "We had a couple of you folks in here just a few months ago. It seems to be a little soon to be stirring up trouble again." He poured the beers and clunked them down on the counter allowing some of the liquid to bounce out of the glass dirtying up the counter.

Jaso took his beer and had a swig without letting his eyes leave the barkeep. Ash thanked the man for the drink as he took his in.

The bartender instantly showed annoyance towards Ash's manners and repeated his question, "How long you staying?" It was a more steadied tone attempting to be threatening to what he perceived as the threat.

Jaso poured the beer down his throat and slammed the

glass back on the counter, "Don't worry. If everything is ship shape, we will be out of here by sunrise."

Ash quickly gulped down his beer attempting to keep up as Jaso was on his feet and walking out the door. They stepped back out into the town and mounted their horses. Ash followed Jaso as he brought his horse up to a full gallop. They went past the buildings in town and reached the farms. There were miles of gardens, stabled animals, and ponds full of fish.

It was not the lush vision he had imagined, but a forced labor camp. The people working the fields and feeding the animals were all gaunt with hunger and bloody from the work. Once they heard the clops of their horses, they stopped what they were doing and watched the two guards as they looked around the farms.

Jaso led Ash up to a small house where they again dismounted and entered. Inside was a small man who looked to be in his early eighties. He was grotesquely skinny and his joints were all swelled past the normal size. He rose to welcome Jaso and show the men to the window where he watched the workers toil away.

He assured the guards that no shipments had been missed and everything was prepared to be sent out before the next full moon to assure the king would not be with a food shortage. When he was asked about the recent freeze, the man swore that all the foods lost were taken from the town's supply, not the king's.

The story being put together in Ash's head was devastating. He could see the poverty and starvation while mass amounts of food were being shipped to Sodorrah. He could not help but think of all the food that was scattered about the city and wasted as the citizens there treated food like a decoration. They never went hungry or passed up the opportunity to use the sustenance for sales or to impress others.

He closed his eyes while listening to the men speak and pictured Ruthie arriving in Sodorrah. He pictured her introduction to prostitution and captivity. She was such a beautiful, intelligent girl who was condemned to use her body to scar her mind with horrid acts. All the promise and greatness of her life was being used up and spit out by others.

He felt sickness rise in his throat and shame sink into his stomach, he did not want to be a guard if this is what he enforced and protected. He hoped that this was the worst of the kingdom.

The old man made them both a bed in the house. He prepared a large feast for the two men and retired for the night with nothing but a blanket on the hard wood floor.

Ash considered what he had seen and tried to push it out of his mind. He ate his fill, laid down on the soft pallet the man had made for him, and closed his eyes with his mind sending him off to sleep with visions of Ruthie.

The comfort of the water had passed. Moshe had returned to feeling the soot of the torch invade his lungs. The lack of sound drove his ears to insanity. They heard nothing but a soft buzz that did not exist. He resorted to speaking his thoughts out loud, but the dryness of his lips caused cracking and bleeding that dripped into his newly sprouting beard.

He tried to moisten his lips with his tongue, but the lack of water had swollen the muscular organ into a large dry pad. The blood did more for his tongue's dryness than it did for any relief from the skin being torn apart in its chapped state.

Lost in time with no view of the outside world he felt his throat begin to close from dryness. As his breathing became a chore of exhaustion he scraped his knuckles against the cold stones to produce more blood. The small trickles of the red life source he used as a way to keep his throat moist enough to maintain use.

He sat in the corner wondering if he could survive when a click echoed in the room that he perceived to be as loud as an explosion. He looked up to see the woman returning to his room with a bucket. She closed the door behind her and quickly scampered over to him. She was the vision of redemption. He felt his life was on a thread and she was his chance. The image of her was that of angel and she would never lose that distinction in his eyes. From that moment he owed her his life and wished he could pledge it to her.

She handed him the bucket full of water and motioned for him to drink. "I have great news my lord. There is talk everywhere of a great king that will rise up to overthrow the fat king. There is panic in the castle, but people from all over the kingdom have been spreading the word. There are rumors of a siege on the palace tomorrow at dawn. When they come I will free you, but until them I am risking everything to speak to you."

Moshe sipped the water and repressed the urge to heave. His body wanted to once again reject the liquid, but as he forced it in little by little he began to feel the water revitalize his body.

The woman looked down ashamed, "I have to take the bucket back, they will see it missing. If you could soak your robes in it you could have water longer." She blushed as she saw him begin to remove his clothes. She turned her back in respect for her new king.

As he dipped his clothing in the water and soaked up the life keeping force as much as he could he asked her, "Please tell me your name."

She hesitated at first, but seemed to decide to oblige her king. "My given name was Mary." She was humbled by his mere desire to hear her name.

"Thank you. I owe you everything." Moshe squatted back in the corner naked and cold. He watched as Mary reached back and retrieved the bucket without turning her head to see him. She walked back out of the room and he was alone again. He was left to thank the lord for sending him an angel as needed as Mary.

Chapter 8

Overthrown

Moshe's mind continued to fight with itself for sanity. There was nothing to pass the time and no way for him to know what was reality at this point. He watched the torch burn, he traced the grooves of the stones, and he smelled the mildew between the walls. He was lost in nothingness.

While he cowered in the corner still sucking water from his soaked robes he heard a crash from outside the palace. It came again. Men ran down the hallway near his door as the booming resounded consistently.

He closed his eyes trying to decide if it was the world around him or the world in his head. The crashing sounded like it was becoming more frequent. He pulled his hands over his ears when he heard the voice of God, "Moshe, now is the time. Prepare to fight for your life, for your people, and for me, your God."

He shook his head to focus on reality and grabbed his half dripping robes. The feel of them was a mix between soggy and slimy. Some of the water had mildewed across the material.

He pulled the robes over his head just as his door unlocked. He looked over to be presented with the sight of Mary. She bore a face wide grin that told him the time had come. She waved her hand for him to follow her and he stumbled as he left the cell.

The hallway was an invasion of the senses. The brightness from the many torches, the sounds of the banging echoing all around him, and the smells of food and activity nauseated his stomach. He pushed through it and fumbled his run down the hallway.

The banging grew louder until it was replaced with the screams of men. Reverberating down the hallway, Moshe could hear the sounds of battle and the screaming's of freedom.

As the turned a corner a large guard seized Mary. He wrapped his forearm around her throat and pulled her into his chest. Moshe stared up at the man in despair as she had been his angel while he was locked up.

The guard pulled his dagger out of its sheath and turned the blade towards the girl's face. "You are the one who was keeping him alive!" The guard's voice was hard and loud.

The woman struggled to free herself, but she was nothing compared to the power of the guard. She closed her eyes as the man slowly moved the blade towards her eye, while staring Moshe down to be sure he did not approach.

Moshe looked on in horror searching his mind for a reprieve for the girl. He slowly stepped towards the scene, but it was received with a quickening of the knife moving inward. He took a step back and the guard laughed as he displayed his yellowed teeth.

As the man leaned over the shoulder of Mary looking to witness the gruesome disfiguration he was about to commit, Moshe saw the bright white light glow from the guard's nose.

He remembered the light leading him through his fight

in the white kingdom and aboard the ship. Looking at the terrified woman he caught her eye and made a slight head jerk motion. Moshe gritted his teeth and made a grunting sound trying to communicate with Mary without giving away the plan.

With another jerk of his skull and a desperate plea of, "now!" he watched the beautiful creature connect with him. She absorbed his thoughts and flung her head back and to the side as hard as she could.

The back of her head crushed into the nose of the guard and he fell back losing his grip on the knife. His feet slipped leaving him crashing into the cobblestoned floor and cracking his skull on the rocks. Deep red oozed from the front and back of his head as he lost consciousness.

Moshe rushed to the girl to find her with a deep wound to her arm, suffered as her attacker fell back. He reached out to comfort her, but she waved him off and took off back down the hallway.

He fought the nervousness and went after her heading straight into the shouting of battle.

Hospitals in Sodorrah were of the nicest in the kingdom. Patricka was confined to a bed in the magisterial hospital. She was still provided with great foods and drinks, but her injuries kept her from being up and about.

Wyndsoria spent the days at her daughter's bedside. They continued to pour through books that she retrieved from the library. Each day they learned bits and pieces of a hidden history no grey skinned person knew about.

Patricka came across a prophecy foretold by ancient men who were among those who glorified technology. The prophecy read, "After God's destruction there will stand only five men who can hear the words of God. Four will rule the

Earth with a false fifth. The four men will speak for their tribes while the fifth will be forgotten. It is he who speaks for the rest of man. He shall not die by the hands of man as he possesses the light of God. It shall happen when the rest of man reawakens to God's word he shall rule the world as one tribe."

The words were nothing, but a jumble to the young girl, but she recognized the word forgotten and held onto the passage as something she should not overlook.

The two sat in the room and read. They paid little attention as the nurses came in from time to time to check on Patricka's broken bones and make sure she was eating. But, midday the second day of her stay the king entered the room.

Wyndsoria barely catching him out of the corner of her eye, immediately bowed her head in respect. Patricka who was not very mobile dipped her head as much as she could hoping not to offend him.

He looked at the girl's splinted body parts and tried to force compassion. It was an odd situation for him. He was accustomed to not having care for his citizens, but with his concubine attached to the girl he felt the need to placate her emotions. If they had not been involved with the forgotten they would receive no such concern. But, the king had grown fond of Wyndsoria and enjoyed playing to her amusement.

He spoke deeply and steady maintaining his magisterial attitude. "I'm sorry to hear of you misfortune, but the business of the kingdom does not cease. Please, tell me what we know of the other king's movements."

Patricka had rehearsed this moment in her head nightly since she received her calling. "Sire, since last I spoke to your admiral there has been no movement militarily on any front. Everyone is watching the disposal of the forgotten."

"And what of it? Has there been any confirmation?"

"No, sire. What we know is that the shipment has

arrived and we are awaiting confirmation of its elimination." She felt proud. She felt accomplished. But, she also felt that she was speaking of her father's death. She had no proof, but as she pieced everything together she was coming to know it as the truth.

The king nodded, "Good, call for me as soon as there is confirmation." He turned to walk out the door, but grabbed Wyndsoria's hand as he passed, "Come, I need a companion, now."

Wyndsoria barely made it to her feet as he dragged her out of the room.

Patricka watched her mother walk away. She considered her fortune to be living as part of the magisterial cabinet, but her thoughts kept falling back to her father. She was afraid the next time she spoke to Devoncote she would be hearing the story of how her dad was disposed of.

As Patricka let her mind ponder such dark things, Wyndsoria had regained her balance and was dutifully following the king briskly walking down the halls of the palace. They passed through the hospital wing and into the magisterial chambers. As she walked over the threshold, he closed the door behind her.

She did as she always did when he requested her presence and disrobed immediately once inside the room. As she lay on his bed he walked through the door in the corner of his room which led into one of his additional sleeping quarters.

She looked at the ceiling being perfectly still. She could feel the king's mood was dark. There was something not going right in his day and it would probably be taken out on her through his sexual aggression. She let her mind wander away so she would not feel the immorality of the afternoon.

She thought of life growing up, life back at Listerbourne, anything to disassociate from the disgusting acts she would perform when he returned.

The door re-opened and the king entered with Genevieve. He held her arm in his hand and shoved her toward the bed as he closed the door behind him.

Genevieve's eyes held an air of disdain as she slowly undid her dress. She swallowed loudly and gasped between breaths.

The king sat on the bed and looked at the women, "No. Wyndsoria, you disrobe Genevieve."

Wyndsoria furrowed her brow and looked at the king with aggravation.

"I want to watch." He leaned back with a vengeful smirk.

Genevieve put her hands on Wyndsoria's wrists and guided her hands around her body to the tie on the back of her dress. The two women pressed their bodies together so she could reach the laces. Genevieve whispered in her ear so the king could not hear, "Ruby and I do this all the time. Enjoy his reaction and forget what you are doing."

Wyndsoria slowly pulled the laces loose and then pulled the dress down over the girls shoulder, "What about Ruby? Why me?"

The woman pulled her arms out of the dress exposing her breasts with other grey skin, "She is with child. It will probably be you and me for a while."

Genevieve lost any soul from her eyes that she had and pressed her mouth against Wyndsoria's. They kissed deeply as she pushed the other concubine to the bed.

They both let their brains leave. There was no thought and no passion, just mechanical submission. The scene was nothing, but a show for the king.

As they tangled into each other's bodies a knock emanated from the door. They did not stop. The king broke his attention from his personal show to deal with the disturbance.

Wyndsoria let her body continue along with her vocal chords, but her mind trained on the door. She moaned with his expectations, but would not focus on the depravity.

The king opened the door to see the head guard standing at attention. He made a brief glimpse to the bed before he bowed his head. "Sire. I apologize, but I have heard some distressing news."

The king looked back at the women who had not slowed their pace and motioned for the guard to continue.

"I have a report saying that the new guard has been less than aggressive in his mission. Jaso has said he seems to be feeling sorrow for your peasants. He is afraid he may rebel against the crown if he continues to learn the inner workings of the kingdom." The words alerted Wyndsoria as she felt it may be Ash who was in trouble. She purposefully increased her pace of degradation, but committed every syllable from the door to memory.

The king shook his head, "No. Continue his mission. Keep him out of the kingdom until the forgotten is gone. Then we can deal with him. I want updates on this though." He started to close the door, but stopped while he watched the women defile each other. Without turning back, "And check the bath house. I want to know what whore he brought into my palace."

As they made their way into the throne room the scene was not the honorable sight Moshe had hoped when he overtook the fat king. There were men lying dead on the ground and the spicy, thick smells of death rose up into his nose where the need to purge his stomach became dire.

Guards had been beheaded and quartered by the citizens who felt they were destroying their oppressors. The fat king sat in his throne wide eyed and helpless. His grotesque form kept him from working towards his own safety.

Five men stood around him with tones of mal intent. Swords were pointed at the man who had already suffered several gashes from his former peasants.

"What am I seeing?" Moshe's voice was wounded, quiet with days of torture. But, the words found their way over the chaos of the room. Everyone seemed to cease their actions and turn to see Moshe gazing upon the scene with terror. His body looked weak and his robes hung from him as if they were a wet towel on a stick.

Mary bowed to the man and stated, "Hail the grey king!"

The room followed suit kneeling to his presence. Clangs of swords hitting the ground rang out as they pulled their focus away from mutilating the bodies of the dead.

Moshe looked over the people in the room and felt he had stepped into something he could not handle, but the voice of God spoke. Moshe repeated the words as they hit his ears.

"We have taken the castle!" Deafening cheers hit the walls of the small room. "As you have defeated those who have been enslaving you, you shall now spread the word of your freedom to others. The lives of these men can be saved. Just because they were the hands of the fat king does not mean they cannot be the hands of the true grey king. Approach all of those who oppressed you with a chance for redemption. If they repent and bow to the one grey skin that can speak with the Lord then they shall live. If they spit on you and condemn you for being led by God himself then they shall not be long for this world. Let them burn in hell with the Devil they worship!" He closed his mouth as the words stopped coming to him.

The room broke out in untimed shouts for the praising of their new king. Men's and women's voices screamed the words "Amen" and "Praise the king".

Moshe held up his hand for them to stop and he said, "No, praise not me. Praise be to God!" Cheers erupted again.

He slowly made his way across the room to face the fat king. The man was turning pale from the loss of blood. His chins wetted with spittle and perspiration. There was nothing but disgust in the appearance of the fat king.

Moshe looked him in his bloated face, "Do you reject your past and accept the future? Do you believe in the one true God and the freedom of his people? Do you bow down to me, the only man in this room who hears the words of God? Do you vow subservience to the grey king?"

Silence fell over the room as the fat man gasped for breath. His eyes slowly made their way up from the ground to the curious grimace of Moshe. He coughed up a few chunks of bloody phlegm as he spoke, "A few days ago the tables were turned. I was the captor and you were the captive. But, nothing has changed as far as who serves who. I am not about to bow down to the forgotten!"

His thoughts were cut short as a sword sliced the former king's throat open. His deep red life force spilled out into his lap draining the remaining color from the fat man's visage.

Moshe looked down on the dying king and said a quiet prayer. He closed his eyes to gain the strength to continue and walked out of the room. He turned the corner of the hallway and exited the building out the side door he came in just days before.

Ash had fallen silent with Jaso. After the first two cities he realized that the entire kingdom was set up to serve the king, not God. The city of Dwellnish existed to produce food for the king and his magisterial cabinet. The second city they visited was the breeding grounds for teachers across the kingdom. While he was there they were bombarded with an uncountable amount of propaganda about the holiness of modern society.

Now he sat upon his steed in the third city, the city of Gamorm, where Ruthie was raised. Every turn through the city's streets he could see her running around as a child enjoying the beauty of her youth. It wasn't a far stretch as the city was filled with children playing about and having no care in the world.

The few adults in the city were just as carefree. There seemed to be no structure or responsibility.

They made their way to the school. It was a small stone building that looked dilapidated. There were only a handful of children walking the darkened halls and no teachers in sight.

As they made each turn through the small hallways Ash held his hand up in case the ceiling caved in on them. But, they reached the main office. It was a small, but pristine room. One wall was half missing leaving full sunshine in and no need for candles or torches.

Jaso talked with the headmaster of the school who was fiddling with some paperwork. It wasn't the sharp noble attitude he used in Dwellnish to keep the farmers in line. And, it wasn't the inquisition he used in New Solundrum when he was speaking to the future teachers of the kingdom. In Gamorm he spoke almost as a therapist trying to convince the befuddled headmaster that he was pushing the kids too hard.

"You have to let kids be kids. Once they are out of here they will receive their callings and there is no more time for play." Jaso gave a half assed frown as he swiveled his head to the sides.

The headmaster nodded and mumbled in agreement as

he gathered papers into neat little stacks.

"I don't want to have any complaints that some of these children made it to their calling and have no good memories because they were stuck in class all day. If God needs them to have vast knowledge, then he will present it to them." Jaso watched the funny little man as he ran his fingers across the edge of the papers trying to line them up perfectly.

The words hit Ash with immense force. This town was not meant to learn anything. They were supposed to be helpless so they would be stuck in menial jobs. Just like his mother was a water bearer. And, just like Ruthie, a prostitute for the lecherous of Sodorrah.

Jaso looked down at the man, the puzzling look on his face questioned if he was all there, "You got it? Hold back the homework."

The man nodded again and pulled out a pointer to check that his papers were aligned perfectly.

Jaso slapped Ash on the back and motioned for him to follow him out. They wound back through the halls and past the couple students. Eventually they found their way back to their horses.

Jaso looked over at Ash, "Might as well make our way to Listerbourne, Gamorm is always the most well behaved of the villages."

Ash put up his best fake learning attitude and asked the questions he hoped he was wrong about. "What do the kids here become? They don't seem to be learning anything."

Jaso looked over at the new guard and carefully chose his words, "Someone has to clean up after the horses. Someone has to fight in the arena. Someone has to work the bath houses. These kids don't know any better so they don't mind when they get there."

He wanted to lash back, he wanted to tell him he was wrong. He had proof. Ruthie, his new found love was not satisfied with being a hooker. She had dreams and aspirations even though she was brought up in this sorry excuse for a town, but he knew better. He knew that as a guard he could not just spout off his opinions to a superior. He held his tongue.

Every step of his travels made him hate the world more. He hated his calling, he hated his king, and he questioned if God was even involved.

He went back to silence as they rode towards Listerbourne. He envisioned his childhood and attempted to analyze it. What was his city a breeding ground for? What were all the children of the town being brainwashed to do?

Outside the Palace of the fat king Moshe looked out at the lush wilderness that was currently peppered with blood and bodies. The mass view of the carnage amongst the celebration was a sickening reality of modern day human kind.

He stood on a balcony at the palace looking down on the gruesome deaths that he had inadvertently caused. His throat seized as he tried to take a breath leaving him to heave over the edge and onto the gore below.

Mary was immediately at his side, caring for him, worrying about him. He appreciated her more than life at that moment. His life was turning out to be death for many others.

She looked at him with eyes glistening in the late day sun. Her grey skin seemed to wash away his illness. "They are expecting a speech." She said as she looked down at the people who began to congregate at the sight of Moshe standing on the balcony. He did not want to speak at that moment, he only wanted to bathe in the refreshing beauty that was Mary.

He was the first man to stand there who was not a fat king. He was the first man to stand there with a woman. He was the first man to stand on that balcony who truly had the support of God.

He looked down at the people, elated with their new realization of freedom. And, although he did hear God speak to him this time he instead spoke with the voice of God, "People of the grey kingdom." Before the echo finished there was a roar that shook the foundation of the palace. "I stand before you not as a new oppressor. I do not stand here today as your new ruler. But, I stand here today as a guidepost to freedom. Today you have overthrown the bounds that held you down here in the fat kingdom. Today you have done away with those who oppose the one true God. Today you have taken back one fifth of your planet!" He felt the cheer building as he spoke. The pause was timed perfectly to allow the crowd to seep some of their excitement out.

"I speak to you not my words, but the words of God. He has told me that we have all been enslaved by kings who do not speak to him. We have been serving men who we claim to be kings, but they in fact worship other Gods! They are the heathens just as bad as the ancients who destroyed this planet with their massive weapons. We are not done. Tonight we freed the fat kingdom, tomorrow we free the black kingdom, then the red kingdom, then the yellow and the white!" He instinctively raised his hands and head to the heavens as the last words screamed past his lips.

"But, hear this! It is God's decree that every man shall be given the chance to recant. Every grey man whether he is rich or a slave shall be given the choice of kneeling before the Lord of the Heavens above or the luxury he built in this hell." Screams resounded up to the balcony as the people grew more wound-up. "If he chooses the almighty then he shall join you hand in hand. If he chooses this world, then do with him as you wish." There was applause beyond comprehension.

He held up his hands until the crowd hushed again. "But be aware we worship our God. He has rejected the people of the kings. Therefore no man who is not grey shall suffer for not worshipping our God. He has deserted them. And so they shall be deserted by us as well. Their destiny is not of concern to our God. If they are allowed to live they shall be sent away from society with a mark upon their bodies. Their skin marks them as rejects, as sinners, as worshippers of false idols."

The crowd responded sporadically, "Praise be to God"

Moshe turned to walk away from the balcony, but Mary was looking at him with awe. Her soul had been swept away by his words.

He laid his hand on her shoulder bringing her back to this world, "We found the spies for the white, black, and red kings. We can send back word to their kingdoms that all is fine and you were killed, but the yellow king."

Moshe nodded. "Yes, spread the word that everything is as it always was. But, I guess this means we start tomorrow in the liberation of the yellow kingdom."

Chapter 9

False Hopes

Patricka was trying to sleep. There was little to do in the hospital and when her mother wasn't around sleeping was the most logical and accessible activity. She had been lying on her bed for half an hour staring at the ceiling when Admiral Devoncote came stomping into the room.

He came in with his typical demeanor, all steadfast and proper as if he was always attending a military function. "Sorry to bother you, but there is new information that can't wait."

Patricka squirmed her butt up the bed trying to sit at attention to give the appearance that she was taking the visit very seriously. She sat up as straight as she could, placed her hands in her lap and looked over at the admiral.

He nodded his approval of her attempt at conformity. "It appears that my fears have come true. The yellow king was able to get his teachers replaced after the explosion at the teaching seminar, but the restock came from the Black King's territory."

Patricka turned her eyes away from the man and nodded

slowly. She didn't know what he was eluding to, but didn't want to give that away.

"The only logical expectation is an attack coming from the Yellow King."

"I will inform our king." Patricka did everything she could to seem professional. "Is there anything else? Word on The Forgotten?" Her words were more forceful than she meant to.

Devoncote let a wicked grin come across his face, he was pleased to see the young girl taking charge. "No official word. There is a rumor from the Yellow King's land that there was some kind of coup against the Fat King, but it isn't from our informant I am waiting to get official word before I can call it intelligence."

He knew the girl was dying for him to leave, so he gathered his hat turned towards the door and marched out. He heard hushed whimpers from the girl as he was leaving, but knowing that she is in a position where she needed to be an adult he kept walking out the door.

Patricka watched him go and was relieved as she couldn't hold in the happiness she felt that her father might still be alive. She looked to the ceiling and thanked God through her tears.

Ash and Jaso rode into Listerbourne early in the morning. It was an odd sight for Ash as he hadn't thought much about his old town since he left. The trail in looked the same as it usually did, lots of dirt and a few huts on the edge of the village.

They came in the same way he left just weeks before. The last memories he had of his home town there had been a party out in the clearing, but now it was just a clearing.

As they slowly trotted in Ash slowed his horse at each

place that housed a memory and peered quietly at each keepsake for his mind. The first to pass was his old house. It did not look like his father was home as the door was closed and no sound seemed to be coming from the structure.

After his hut they passed the blacksmith and butcher. He smiled and waved at the two men working their callings, but he was not received with joyous salutations back. Instead he was met with confused stares and voiceless gaping mouths. Ash did not question anything as he had rarely seen guards inside the edges of his village and assumed the sight of two guards was awe inspiring and possibly frightening to a people who had just had three of their citizens sent off to the capital.

They continued down the old dirt road passing Ash's school, but that was not the place that Ash wanted to go. He knew his father was at work. He must be preparing his sermon for the next service. "Sir?" Ash asked turning towards Jaso.

"Yes?" Jaso did not swivel his head to refocus his attention.

"Are we headed to the church?"

"Yes, it is the focus of this town."

Hearing this swelled a lump of pride within Ash's abdomen. He had always cared for his father and appreciated what he did, but to hear that his calling was the focus of the town's purpose made him feel especially proud.

But, he was too joyous to realize that the church was the focus of the town because it created citizens who had a purpose. It made dedicated and dutiful workers for the king. The citizens of Listerbourne made wonderful guards, advisors, soldiers, tax collectors, ship captains…

They rode up to the church and Ash couldn't get his horse tied up quick enough. He was racing against physics to get dismounted and in the door.

He burst in through the front doors and excitedly charged down the aisle between the pews. As he raced behind the altar to the staircase in the back he noticed the green banners hanging from the both the altar and above the high windows.

He leapt two and three steps at a time until he reached the top of the staircase and bounded down the hallway across the green carpet. As he started to push the door open he realized that all the adornments should not be green. For the religious festivals coming up things should be adorned in purple. As the door opened to show a stranger sitting at his father's desk he remembered what green symbolized… A new priest.

"Who are you?" Ash couldn't stop the words from coming out.

"Father Fairow." He stood up to shake the guard's hand. "I am the new priest, since the last one was sold off to the Fat King."

"He was," Ash took in a deep shaking breath as he tried to comprehend the words. "Sold?" He turned around with his back to Father Fairow to remove himself from the sight, but instead he was treated to a view of Jaso, now standing in the doorframe his eyes looking at the ground and his head just slightly shaking.

Ash stomped over to his superior allowing his armor to clang about through the cavernous house of God. He looked up into the eyes of the boy he currently loathed. "You knew?"

There was no answer which told him everything he needed to know. He stepped past Jaso and back into the hallway banging his shoulder plate against Jaso's. He walked past all the green decorations again, but this time their meaning seemed to scream out at him. And, he walked out the door.

Wyndsoria sat in the corner of the concubine's quarters staring out the window. The view was immaculate. Peering over the outer wall of the palace and down the hill, she could see all the rooftops of Sodorrah. But, no matter how hard she tried, her mind wouldn't allow her to focus on the beauty of the scenery for very long. As she tried to tell herself that the view was the most glorious she would ever have the chance to see, the phantom touch of Genevieve would graze across her skin and a tear of loss would build in her eye.

Each time it happened she shuddered in disgust of her experience. It wasn't that she was repulsed by the touch of Genevieve per say, but the fact that the king orchestrated it, watched it, and expected it was what gave her the chills. She also knew that sometime in the next day or so he would call on her. She dreaded that moment. Wyndsoria did not know whether or not she could bring herself to disrobe and present herself to him. Or worse he may bring her and Genevieve in together again.

She crossed her arms in front of her and grasped her shoulders as she looked out over the scenery again when she jumped from a hand softly touching her shoulder. Her eyes fell to the floor knowing it must be the king. A deep breath prepared her as she turned to face her tormenter, but it was not the king. Ruby stood just behind her with a sympathetic face.

Her voice was soft and shameful as tried to comfort Wyndsoria. "I am sorry for what you went through."

Wyndsoria was taken aback. She had very little interaction with Ruby and assumed the woman wanted nothing to do with her. "Thanks?" The response came out as a question, but was meant to be a statement.

"The first time is hard."

Wyndsoria tilted her head and looked back out the window before she got the nerve to question Ruby. She turned back and looked the soon mother to be in the eye. "What is this? I know you don't like me."

Ruby fought back her own tears as she looked up nodding her head. "I am sorry. I deserve that. I don't dislike you. I was afraid you would replace me."

"Well, I don't want to be your replacement. You can have it. You can run off with Genevieve and perform your little sex show for that bastard!" Tears began to flow freely. "I was torn from my kids. My husband is most likely dead. I have no freedom over my own body or actions."

Ruby kneeled down next to Wyndsoria. She rubbed the woman's back and lowered her tone to a whisper. "I am sorry. I am. You are a good person I am sure. And I remember how demeaning that first experience can be."

"It's not just doing it. But, he seemed like he cared about me! And while I was being forced to pervert for his entertainment he was talking about my son! My son and a whore…" Her words trailed off as Ruby pulled her in close. The warmth of the two bodies brought the slightest amount of comfort.

They swayed side to side slowly, Ruby hushed any words that peeked their head out and tried to soothe in any way she could. The two women cried together not knowing what they could do for one another. But, the moment did more than anything else could have at that time.

In the end the concubines stood up for each other. Ruby helped Wyndsoria to bed, rubbed her back, and told her it would all be ok. Genevieve told the guards outside the door that Wyndsoria was coming down with something and the king should be given word that he may become ill if he takes her tonight. And the older woman fetched soup from the kitchen for her.

Wyndsoria did not heal her psyche over night, but she found herself surprised with her feelings towards people. Her views of Genevieve, Ruby and the king had all made an about face. She realized the sacrifice Genevieve was making, if Ruby was undesirable because she was pregnant and Wyndsoria was sick, then the only person the king would use would be Genevieve.

But, Ruby's sacrifice wasn't lost either. Wyndsoria remembered being pregnant and the idea that Ruby would push that aside to comfort a stranger was truly moving.

Moshe had made the palace of the fat king his home base. He went up to the balconies to speak to his people every few hours, but the rest of the time he was down in the throne room with the people who had led the rebellion.

The main players were Mary who rarely left his side, Loht who had spread the word throughout most of the markets near the town they landed in, and Buz who was responsible for the majority of the message's infiltration in the fat king's personal defense force.

Although it had only been about a day since they had usurped the fat king, Moshe felt that he was constantly being bombarded by the requests of Loht and Buz to create a strategy for invading the yellow king.

Walking into the throne room again Moshe saw that Loht and Buz had acquired the map that he had been requesting. They were standing in the center of the room with the large map of the world sprawled out across the stone floor. Both of them carried what seemed to be permanently idiotic looks on their faces.

Moshe took a deep breath as he approached the men and pointed over towards the throne signaling Mary to give him some space. She nodded and sped up her walk to join the boys on what was about to be the audience side of the throne room. As she walked in front of Moshe, he noticed the beautiful profile of her face and how the glimmering shadows of the torches made her look like the definition of beauty. Her strong cheekbones and slim nose gave her a feminine look that drew Moshe in. It was something that happened more and more, but Moshe was fighting it. He told himself he was married to Wyndsoria and she would be waiting for him to return, but as Mary lined up on the other side of the room the empty space by his side left Moshe feeling alone again.

As he approached the rug sized map on the ground and the two men with dumbfounded looks and excitement to match, he asked aloud, "What exactly arc you hoping I can tell you now?"

Loht looking a bit surprised retorted almost immediately. "We need to know what to do. You said we were about to invade the yellow king's land and you were going to lead us to free the rest of the people across the lands and…"

Moshe held up a hand to cut off the man from rambling on. He kneeled down on one knee and looked at the map. He pointed to the fat king's land and said, "We are here." Pointing to their location near the top of the map, he looked over at the yellow king's territory which was connected by land to the south. "And, this is where we need to go."

Sighs of frustration came from Loht and Buz. Buz began to worry about the man he put all his hopes and faith behind. "I thought you spoke to…" He stopped talking as he looked down at the map. Thousands of tiny lights had lit up across the lands of the map. Thousands and thousands of grey pinpoints were shining in each of the king's lands. There were also white, red, yellow, and black dots that showed up mostly in the capital cities of the lands.

Moshe nodded his head and looked to the sky to silently

thank his God for showing him the plan. He looked back down at the map and watched as the battle plan play out in front of him. Although the majority of the grey lights started out in the land of the fat king they mostly migrated down south to the yellow king's land. As they did they grouped up into the small outer cities of the territory. As those lights showed up in those cities the few yellow dots either went out or turned grey. Some of them spread out to the west and across the oceans to the red, black, and white kingdoms. There they turned more and more colorful dots to grey.

Then some grey dots from across the ocean at the white king's capital moved towards the yellow capital at the same time a large grey dot moved down from where Moshe was currently kneeling to the yellow capital. Once both groups of grey dots converged with almost all the red, white, and black lights gone, there was an explosion of yellows and greys at the yellow capital. Suddenly, all the light on the map disappeared and Moshe looked up at Loht, Buz, and Mary. "Understand?"

Mary looked at the two men and stated, "Go spread the word. We need to move at once, get our people into the outer cities of the Yellow Kingdom and spread the word of the Grey King!"

The hut was still empty. Since Ash's entire family had been removed from Listerbourne no one had come and taken their place. He sat alone in his old room just staring at the light that seeped in through the wooden slats. He didn't know why his father had been sold, but he understood now that his calling was one of convenience.

He felt like an imbecile. He should have put the puzzle pieces together. His young sister was sent her calling years before normal, he received his on the same day. Then his mother happens to be honored in the city where he and his sister were while his dad is nowhere to be found. He wished he could return to the previous few weeks and just be a kid with a family.

Deep breathing didn't help him so he tried kicking the dirt around under his bed, but playing in the dirt floors did nothing either. As he questioned his intelligence for not seeing that something odd had happened he heard footsteps coming from the living area. He turned and faced the doorway to see Jaso emerging in to the threshold.

Ash turned back and returned to his fiddling with the dirt on the ground.

Jaso spoke out in a less authoritative voice than normal. "I'm sorry, I just didn't know what to say. I thought maybe seeing that the rest of your town was still intact might cushion the blow."

Ash chuckled a laugh of incredulity.

"I know that you grew up here, so you aren't aware of certain things and the longer you stay in Sodorrah the more you will learn about things that not commonly spoken in the rest of the kingdom."

Ash blew out a loud shaky breath. "You don't have to do this. I just wanted to be alone anyway."

"No, you need to understand what has happened. You can't possibly move on without knowing."

Ash stood and walked past Jaso and out the door. Jaso followed his subordinate out to the field behind the hut.

Ash looked up at the sky and screamed, "Why have you taken my father?" A twinkle appeared just over the horizon of the midday sun.

Jaso put a hand on the boy's shoulder, "Just listen." He took a deep breath and spoke to the back of Ash's head. "There is a prophecy that is widely talked about in Sodorrah. It is forbidden knowledge from all the other towns. It is called the forgotten. I don't know the actual text, but it speaks of a grey that can speak to God. And it speaks of this grey that will destroy the world as we know it."

Ash fell to his knees onto the desert floor. He shook his head slowly and instinctively as Jaso continued his lesson, "I know you loved your dad. And, I understand that this is a shock, but it is for the betterment of mankind and our world." He paused looking out at the star that was still blinking on the horizon. "Look, there are signs that someone might be the forgotten. Have you ever seen him speak to God?"

Ash turned and looked up at Jaso, "He was priest for crying out loud!"

"No, Ash. I mean have you ever seen him speak to God and then hear God in return? Have you ever seen him create miracles? Have you ever seen him engulfed in light?"

Ash crooked his neck and as he looked at the boy. The moment where he watched the stars change with his dad sprang to mind. There was no denying it was a miracle and Moshe had explained it as God speaking to them.

"Ash, these are parts of the prophecy. These are the things that the destroyer of our world can do. These are the reasons the kings must capture and…" Once again Ash cut off his superior from fear of hearing the actual words.

Ash returned to his feet and started to walk back to the center of town. "Can we just finish up here and get on to the next town?"

Still playing sick, Wyndsoria was taking a risk by going out into the city. She was ever grateful for what the other girls had done for her, but she couldn't live with the knowledge that the king had accidentally bestowed upon her.

She had walked alone nearly half way down the hill to

reach the part of the road which had the bath house. She knew the king had said Ash brought a whore into his castle, but she didn't know anything else. After some talking with Ruby she decided to try the bath house. It was the place where girls who calling was to serve men's sexual fantasies worked.

The front of the building was quite extravagant. It was tall with four large circular pillars. Over the top of the quartet of columns was a triangular stone with bath house etched into it.

She climbed the stairs and entered the building. Once inside she was greeted by a scrawny man who wasn't quite sure what to think of her. He looked her up and down, stopped, and then did it again. He opened his mouth to tell her something when he realized what scarf she was wearing. It was a magisterial scarf showing that she was a part of the king's court. He gasped from the sight of the insignia and immediately changed his demeanor. Suddenly he wanted nothing more than to make this woman happy.

His voice came out a bit screechy and high. "How can I help you my dear?"

Wyndsoria wasn't sure what to say. She had no actual plan, but to find the girl that the king had accused Ash of bringing into the castle.

"It is ok my dear. I understand. We can be discreet. Let me take you to the choosing room and you can have any woman you desire." He came up right next to Wyndsoria and put his arm around her waist nudging her towards the choosing room door.

She reached down into the satchel strapped to her leg, but she was intercepted by the manager of the club. "No, no, no. Your money is not accepted here. You are a part of the magisterial court and as a part of the king's court your money is no good here. He pushed her to the door and opened it up to reveal the choosing room.

The sight of the couple dozen women all nude and lounging around in the room was slightly sickening to her. It brought back her humiliation of being forcefully taken by another woman. She felt ill and sorry for all the women in the room. She quickly understood that the inhumanity that she endured from the mind of the king was only the depravity of one man while these women would endure the same humiliation day and night, but it would be by the hands of dozens if not hundreds of men.

She choked down the terror she was feeling at that moment and attempted to look interested. She looked around the room trying to guess who Ash would have wanted to be with, but came up empty. She looked the little man in the face and asked, "Which girl is it that the king's guard took to the castle?"

The small man looked over at her and very sternly replied. "Madame. That is an egregious accusation. I don't appreciate it."

"I'm sorry, maybe he didn't take her out of here I must be mistaken. I am wanting the girl that the magisterial guard Ash had spent some time with." She hoped her new attempt at diplomacy would calm the man.

"My apologies madam, but the girl you speak of, Ruthie, she has been spoken for. For quite a few days actually. I can't deliver her to you as she is in a private space right now. But, let me get you a good time on the house."

Wyndsoria was sad and confused. She shook her head, turned, and walked out the door without saying another word to the little man.

Chapter 10

Setup

Patricka was regretting asking the king for another meeting. She knew that she had to tell him about the attack from the yellow king, but she wished it had already been done. She was happy to be out of the hospital, even if her entire body was sore from traveling to king's personal office while she was still not over her injuries.

She was very happy to be out of the hospital bed and experiencing the world of the healthy. As she sat and waited for the king she watched the birds chirp outside, bouncing from stone to stone on the outer wall of the palace. It was a scene of contentment. Something that she had not experienced over the last couple weeks. They were just shy of the winter weather taking over and driving the birds to warmer ground leaving the rest of the animals to fend off the cold for their own survival.

It wasn't a long time looking out into the beauty of nature that the king walked in behind Patricka. Although she had no way of noticing him, he was visibly annoyed that she was not on her feet as he walked into the room.

He cleared his throat loudly and Patricka jumped out of her chair. She turned to face her leader while dropping her eyes to the gorgeous rug that warmed the room.

"You show about as much respect as your brother." The king's eyes were laser focused on the young girl. "I don't know what it is about your family, but I am your ruler, your lord, and your savior! When I walk in a room I expect to be treated as such!"

Patricka fell back into the role of the little girl she actually was. Tears rolled down her cheek while she muttered at the ground, "I'm sorry sire."

"What is it that drug me halfway across my palace to see you?" He leaned over his desk both arms straight, hands planted on the wood. His eyes had not moved from his locked gaze.

"Sire. I learned that… Admiral Devoncote told me…" The sentences kept breaking up between the sobs.

His demeanor softened, not out of sympathy, but out of the annoyed realization that if he didn't the girl wasn't going to get through her statement. "Calm down. I am just making sure you understand your place. Now, take your time and tell me what I need to know."

Patricka finally looked up at the man with his fake grin on his chubby, sweaty face. She took a deep breath and proceeded. "Sire, I have been informed that the yellow king has made a transaction with the black king. In exchange for a shipment of teachers the yellow king has agreed to attack your kingdom as payment to the black king." She let a quick stream of breath in excitement that she completed her duty.

The king slammed one fist into the desk startling Patricka. He swung around the desk and headed for the door. "Garbage!" he mumbled as he made his way out of the room.

Patricka swung around to stand at attention while he left and saw one of the golden guards at the door. As the king passed him the guard walked with his king.

"Yellow is planning an attack." The conversation started as Patricka quickly skittered behind to try and hear. "Bring everyone in, we need to be preemptive on this. We attack immediately at their capital!"

The guard nodded his head as he replied, "The intensity of the yellow king and his army will be too much for any of our troops. This is a suicide mission."

"I am aware. But, so is the yellow king. If we can attack first we may keep the battle on his turf and sustain no casualties at home."

The guard responded very matter of fact, "But, the source? You believe her?"

"She is scared to death. Yes, I do. Her brother may be trying to hide things from me, but I trust her, for now."

The two's pace was too great and Patricka fell behind. It may have been her injuries or that she was trying to keep undetected, but she couldn't keep up anymore.

The night had just begun to darken the sky when Jaso stopped his steed and squinted at the horizon. Ash slowed down to mimic his superior. As they both looked out into the nothingness Ash thought he saw an explosion. It was a few inches above the horizon and they could barely make it out.

Just as Jaso was about to say something an incredible boom came from behind him. It was another explosion, but this time over the city of Listerbourne. They both turned around to look and they saw another explosion very high in the air creating a sort of crisscross pattern that was lit up with a bright orange shimmer. The echoing sounds spooked the horses causing them to sidestep a few feet.

Ash looked over to Jaso in panic, "What is happening?"

He was already soothing his horse and preparing to charge straight back to Listerbourne.

"It's a signal. We must return to Sodorrah." Jaso began looking to the sky to orient himself with his cardinal directions.

"But, what about my town? I need to go back and save my friends."

"No, everyone you know is fine. This is a sign from Sodorrah to call all guards to return home. It travels from town to town as they see neighboring groups setting off the signal. Don't worry about Listerbourne, the king needs us back at the capital.

The two boys turned to head towards the brightest star in the sky. The horses trotted along at an unhurried pace and Ash looked to his right to watch the explosions continue over his old home.

"Why have I never seen this before?" Ash was still concerned and did not want to abandon his old friends.

"I've never seen it before either. It has been a very long time since a king has signaled all his reports back to Sodorrah. The last time was when the last king died and his son became king. That was before either of us were around. Which means something serious must be happening." Jaso's voice was dark and cold, his fear of what the current situation was bled through to his tone.

Ash didn't speak for a while. He let the wind of the desert play with his mind. But, as he remained silent his brain questioned his calling. After everything he had seen at the different villages within the kingdom and the obvious deficiencies that each location had, how could he trust that he was to be a guard. As much as he believed his entire life that God would take care of him and guide him, he now could only see the king guiding his life.

After an hour of silent travel Ash spoke up, "Jaso? I am

having trouble understanding how God can allow some of the things I've seen recently."

"That is a question for a priest. I know not of God's plans." Jaso almost said the words with a chuckle.

"The what of the king? How can he create these cities where children are bred for a purpose? Where they believe they are living a full life with all their decisions ahead of them, but they aren't. They are born into a process where they become what the city has designed for them."

"It must be done. If we don't have training grounds for the next group of soldiers then no one will be willing to risk their lives. If we don't have people who we know are going to train the youth then we won't have teachers. You are saying it isn't the will of God, but why isn't it? How do you know that God is not delivering the correct people to the correct villages?"

"I don't know there is a God choosing anything. All I can see is our king developing our lives. We are born into a production line that is shaping the rest of our lives for its purpose."

"Watch your tongue if you want to remain a free man." The warning was a show of friendship from the older boy. If those words had been spoken while in Sodorrah Ash would have been thrown in a dungeon at best and his head paraded around on a stick at worst.

"Sorry Jaso. I don't mean to put you in a bad situation."

Jaso nodded and pulled up on the reigns on his horse. "Fine, but we need to camp now." He said as he dismounted his horse landing on the hard desert floor that would be his bed for the night.

"There come times in mankind's history where courage is a necessity. Those times have much at stake and God asks his people to put their fears aside and take what is rightfully theirs. Today we have reached one of those moments. Soon, many of you will be faced with a former king or invading army that may threaten your life or lively hood. Do not stand down! Do not falter! Take your freedom that God intended and the Kings of One Color have stolen from you!" The end of the speech came out in a roar that echoed down from the balcony which Moshe stood on.

The crowd cheered their leader and chanted the praises of their savior. Moshe didn't know if they worshipping their true lord or himself. But, as long as the movement continued to spread he was willing to accept the inappropriate praise.

As he turned back to re-enter the palace, Mary held up his robes to keep them from dragging on the ground. He returned inside and traveled past the throne room and to his personal quarters.

Mary followed him in still carrying the bottoms of his robes. He turned around to dismiss her, but she asked if she could wash his feet. The request was soft and almost childlike, but he could feel a yearning behind it that felt wrong. But, Moshe had built such a care for the woman he could not deny her when something appeared to matter so much to her.

He nodded to her as he retired to his chair. Mary left the room to fetch a bowl and water. While she was gone Moshe was distraught with confusion.

He bent forwards holding his head trying to envision his wife. Wyndsoria's springy curled hair and strong jawline were almost invisible to him now. He had gone weeks without seeing her and had lost the image that was burned into his mind. Every time he tried the features would morph. The jawline would soften, the cheekbones would rise and the eyes would open with a brightness. And as he tried to picture the woman he pledged his life to he would find himself picturing the woman who was now there for him at all times.

Mary returned to the room with a steaming bowl of water. He looked up to see her sheepish smile as she slid in around the door frame. She kneeled at his feet and dipped the sponge into the hot water. As she began to wash his left foot, softly wiping the dirt from the sole, she looked up and caught his eye. The wantonness behind her gaze gave Moshe the chills.

He closed his eyes and spoke to God within his mind. He asked why he had brought Mary to him. His life was devoted to Wyndsoria and did not understand why God would tempt him with a woman who was so loving and giving.

Before he opened his eyes he heard the voice of God. "Moshe, you did not pledge your life to Wyndsoria in my name. Your marriage was in recognition of the white king. As she has revoked her vows to you, you shall revoke your vows to her. But know, if you give yourself to another under my blessing there shall be revocation."

With that Moshe opened his eyes with a smile. He looked down at the woman kneeling before him with a different light. "Mary, please come here."

"But sire, I am not finished. Please, let me do this for you." Her voice soft and subtle.

Moshe's heart was softened at the dedication to him. He silenced his objections and let her continue. He decided as he watched her that he must return the favor. He must show her that he should not be worshipped, but that they should as people take care of one another. As much as the gesture moved him he could not be seen as above her or anyone else.

When she finished she bowed her head and tried to leave the room, but Moshe took her by the hand. He turned her back to face him and slid out of his chair to his knees. As he kneeled before her he apologized. "Mary, thank you. That was the most selfless act and I have not been good to you. I am sorry I have treated you like a servant, but I was afraid of my own motives. God has spoken to me and released me from my own fear. Please understand we are equals and serving me is not necessary."

Mary looked down into her king's eyes and she smiled. "I understand."

Wyndsoria returned to the concubine's quarters ashamed of trying to interfere in her son's life. She did not know what was happening in her world. Everything she thought she knew was crumbling around her.

She saw Ruby and Genevieve sleeping in the corner and went over to see if Ruby would talk to her. She had been so nice the other day she thought maybe she had found a real friend in this backwards city.

She tapped the girl on the shoulder who gently drifted into the conscious world. Ruby looked up into the eyes of Wyndsoria and immediately felt there was something wrong. Softly and a bit hoarse she asked, "What is wrong, dear?"

Wyndsoria, so pleased to hear such a nice question let out a huge smile. "When I got out of the castle for a bit, I did something I shouldn't have." Wyndsoria replied with excitement.

Ruby pulled herself upright to focus on the story without the desire to return to her slumber.

"I went to the bath house looking for the girl that Ash brought to the palace." She bowed her head in humility as she knew it was out of line for her to do such a thing. "I wanted to meet this girl. I don't know what I was going to do. I might have wanted to scold her, maybe just meet her, maybe find out what he did with her, although I couldn't hear that, it would be terrible."

Ruby reached over and pulled Wyndsoria in and placed the woman's head on her chest. She gently rocked back and forth. Her maternal instincts were getting stronger as the pregnancy moved along.

Wyndsoria mumbled to no one in particular complaining about the king, her son, the pressure her daughter felt… The blubbering was loud enough that it awoke Genevieve who lay there quietly trying not bring attention to herself. Instead she just lie there listening to the lack of dedication to their king.

After a few minutes of the crying and sobbing the door burst open. The sound of it hitting the stone wall startled all three girls. They all craned their necks to see what the commotion was and it was the king with one of his guards.

He looked down his nose trying to see over the furniture. Wyndsoria got on all fours peaking her face over the back of the bed Ruby had been leaning against and presented her bright red face, painted from her uncontrollable sob session. The king let out an audible grunt of disapproval. When Genevieve poked her head up over the back of her headboard the king motioned to her, "Genevieve, come with me." He held out a hand to the girl as she made her way across the room to her lord. "Wyndsoria, this is your last reprieve. Next time I don't want any excuses."

Genevieve skipped over to the king and took his hand. As they walked out across the threshold the king's concubine whispered just loud enough for the girls to hear, "I think you might want to know." She paused as she looked back over the king's shoulder, "Someone's been naughty."

Ash shivered as he lay in the cold night of the desert. He grew up in the area, but he did not spend nights outside of his hut. Trying to sleep on the dirt with the random wind gust that stung the skin with flying sand was a feat in its own right.

His mind was still wrapped with the pain of what he had seen, the fear of what his father was, and the sadness for everything that he had lost. Everything was too much to deal with. His new hatred for the king was something that was unwavering. The idea that Ruthie was damned to be a prostitute because the king had bred her to be such was disgusting and something he could never forgive.

But, the idea that the king was doing such evil made him wonder if the story he heard about his father was wrong. Maybe his father was not evil and going to destroy the world, but how could he know. The only answer was with God if god even existed.

He thought back to the day when his father spoke to God and the stars moved. He had seen it multiple times now, but he didn't know if it was God or his father that was making these things happen. Could his father be this forgotten thing and have powers that most men couldn't comprehend?

Ash gave in. He stood up and quietly walked out into the desert to get away from Jaso. Each step was a small journey towards a lonely spot where he might be able to feel the whole of God as that would be the only being occupying the space with him.

He traveled out until he almost couldn't make out where Jaso and the horses were. Then he stood up looking directly up and into the sky. He spoke aloud, "God, you showed yourself to my father. I need you to show yourself to me." The wind softly blew splattering sand particles into Ash's cheek. He reached his arms out and took a deep breath trying to find that connection to the divine that he needed to feel.

As Ash reached out to the point where his arms ached and he was ready to give up there was a star far in the distance, almost invisible to the naked eye, that suddenly glowed. It started to increase in brightness until it was the brightest star in the sky. Then without warning it separated into dozens of stars with a brilliant dark purple and red haze that connected them all. It was an amazing site that was well beyond Ash's comprehension.

The display could have only been the work of God and Ash began laughing with gratitude. His arms still spread and his head faced upward he began shouting. "Thank you lord! Thank you for your sign!" He fell to his knees in respect and bowed his head to continue his conversation with the deity. "Please help me. What am I supposed to do? Is my father evil? Is he the forgotten?"

A voice as full as the desert was empty rang in Ash's ears. "Son, your father is a good man. He is the messenger of my word as you are the messenger of my word. What the kings call the Forgotten, is nothing more than a prophecy they do not wish to live through. It refers to a family of people who will lead the world to the return of my worship. The world now is an abomination just as it was in ancient times when men put development over me. Today the kings have put their own greed over me and it will not last forever. There is a family, a bloodline, that will overthrow the kings. This prophecy was foretold hundreds of years ago and for hundreds of years I have been trying to lead this family to this future. You are of this bloodline. Your father is also of this bloodline."

Ash gasped in shock. He did not know how it was possible that his father was actually his birth father. "But, lord. I was chosen by my father, how could he be…"

God cut him off, "Just as I control the natural forces of this world I can also lead man to make certain decisions. You and your father are true father and son. It is now the two of you I will lead to the destiny. But, just as the men before you, there is free will and without faith and courage you will be lost to history like your ancestors."

"Tell me what to do."

"Return to Sodorrah. Follow the king's orders, but remember you are in this world to free your fellow man. Once you embark do not hide your true purpose from your fellow man."

As soon as the words finished filling Ash's ears he knew God was finished. The desert which had just felt so warm and full of life was once again a cold dark place where he was all alone. He nodded his acceptance of his mission, thanked God, and slowly walked back to Jaso.

Chapter 11

Scars

The gala was another glorious event. Just as the one, weeks beforehand there was entertainment, food, dancing, and guests of honor. This time the event was in honor of six people who all completed their calling. Patricka watched on from the sidelines. Being a part of the magisterial court she was invited to all the balls and galas held in the palace, but she was quickly understanding why she may not continue to attend them.

It was the same entertainment as before. The same jester, the same speeches, and the same music as when her mother was honored. The only real difference was an occasional explosion shot off into the night sky. From the ballroom they could see a small amount of the sky and every so often there was a large explosion that made for a beautiful sight. Patricka was surprised how something as violent as an explosion could be so beautiful.

The people being honored all seemed a bit awkward. A couple were lanky while another was quite fat. Most were balding in an unflattering way. They just had the appearance of general misfits.

When Patricka first arrived there seemed to be a customary number of officials there. She and Devoncote were standing along the long wall looking important. There were a half dozen other advisors mingling amongst themselves.

Over by the table of honored guests were the cooks and servers as expected and at each of the entrances there were a couple of guards. But, as the night went on the number of guards grew and it grew quickly.

After being distracted by the sky explosions she looked up and the number of guards had doubled. And nearly a quarter of them were in golden armor. It wasn't common to see so many golden guards as they were the leaders of small platoons, but it was typically the iron clad low level guards that had to deal with the public.

She started to count realizing that they went from the initial eight to sixteen, then within minutes there were twenty five, then thirty nine. She was glad she was on the right side of the king as this looked like a bad sign for anyone who opposed him.

Moshe sat in the throne looking down at his map with the lights of God dancing across it. As amazing as it was to watch God broadcast the movements of the troops, it was aggravating not being able to affect any of it.

He watched with Mary standing by his side, leaning on his shoulder. He pointed to the kingdoms of the red and black kings, "Look, the message is spreading quickly in the farther away lands. Why is the capital of the yellow king not turning grey?"

Giving Moshe a gentle pat on the back, "I do not know. We can see that they have infiltrated all the outside villages."

She was right, the yellow lights in all the villages on the outskirts of the yellow kingdom had changed to grey, but the bright lights in the cluster where his capital city was remained unchanged.

He swiped his hand over the map and everything reset. He could see that his people had already taken over the outer towns of the yellow lands. As he watched the events unfold in light he could see the red and black kings would fall to the grey movement within days. The white kingdom remained white with the exception of a few small grey lights. Those greys were engulfed by a very bright white light that sailed across the sea to the yellow land. But, the grey movement never moved towards the yellow capital.

"Damnit!" Moshe stood up while also stomping his foot to create a booming echo in the small throne room.

Mary was immediately up and trying to sooth the man, "It is ok, we will figure this out."

"No! This isn't a matter of figuring it out. I need to be out there, I need to lead our people into the yellow palace, they are stalling for some reason and I don't know what that is. If I go out there I can convince them."

Mary was appalled at the idea that Moshe would risk his life by going out to the battle lines. She tried to convince him that it was unnecessary, but it was not working.

When Moshe went to his room to find some clothes for travel, Mary ran down the corridor and found Loht and Buz. She drug them back to the throne room where Moshe was once again poring over the map.

Loht spoke up, "I just wanted to say that I don't think you getting killed is going to help the cause." His low voice made him sound a bit like an idiot.

Moshe looked up at the man. "You really think that is my plan? Look at the damn map! All of our troops are stalled. What do you think happens if we just sit here and wait for them to accomplish their mission?" As if he had just commanded it, the map reset with a huge flash of light that swept across the lands.

The map once again showed the outside villages of the yellow king grey. They all watched as the grey lights ventured out and turn the black and red lights to grey. The lights from the white kingdom arrived at the shores of the yellow and there is a standstill for a few minutes. Then the lights in the red and black kingdom started to return to red and black. They began to move across the map towards the yellow castle. The convergence of red, black, white, and grey outside the yellow castle all started sparking.

The black lights went out, the red lights went out, then the white started to charge against the grey front. As that happened the yellow lights started to pour out of the castle. They all moved north to the grey castle where the grey lights quickly started to fade out. The brightest yellow and white lights went to the center of the grey castle and the brightest grey light dwindled. Then all the grey lights turned back to white.

Moshe looked up at Loht and stated very firmly, "Fine, if we stay here we all die. Is that enough motivation for you?"

Moshe stood and headed towards the door while the others shrugged and followed their leader.

Ruby and Wyndsoria had spent most of the day in each other's arms. Wyndsoria would speak of the harshness the king had shown her and Ruby would speak of the difficulties of pregnancy. They gave each other exactly what they needed at the time and their day had brightened up quite a bit.

As Wyndsoria was petting Ruby's hair and looking down at the beautiful features of the young woman another bang came into the concubine's quarters. The both spun around not sure what they would find. Genevieve hadn't returned and they didn't expect to see the king before her. As the door swung out of the way, there stood a guard.

"Wyndsoria. Concubine of the king. Please come with me." The guard spoke with utter perfection and no hint of actual interest.

She stood up and straightened up her dress before she raised her chin in the air and walked to the doorframe like a proper lady. She walked out the door in front of the guard with no questions or assistance.

They walked briskly down the hallways of the palace, the guard jogging up in front to show her the way. Both of them treated the situation as a normal required piece of their lives. There was no small talk, no wavering or stuttering, it was business to the end.

They curled around hallways and bends until they reached the king's quarters. This was the first time that Wyndsoria showed any signs of hesitation. She took a couple deep breaths as the guard stood beside her and bowed down waiting for her to enter the room. She nodded and then pushed the two large oak doors open.

She glided in with her head up and arms floating up beside her. She meant to make some lewd comment about being prepared for the king and his "staff", but something caught her eye. She noticed a small girl standing beside the king's bed. She was naked and staring at Wyndsoria.

"Sire? Who is this?" Wyndsoria lost the act, she was no longer being proper.

The king stood up and walked over to Wyndsoria. He reached down and grabbed her dress and slowly pulled it up over her head. Afterwards, she was standing in his room wearing only her knickers and brazier. He reached to her side and unsnapped the brazier peeling it off her soft skin. He leaned over and pulled her knickers down to the floor exposing her to himself and the girl.

He took her very gently by the hand and slowly guided her over to the bed where the girl stood, almost shaking. Once he had the two of them face to face. He placed a hand behind the neck of each girl and guided them into a kiss together.

As they performed the task their king desired he smiled, and spoke with a bit of gusto. "I would be happy to introduce you." He pushed the women forward leading Wyndsoria to lay on the bed and the other woman to straddle her while they continued the lecherous deed. "This is Wyndsoria, the mother of Ash. And, Wyndsoria, this is Ruthie the good for nothing whore your son was parading around my kingdom!"

Both women gasped at the realization of what was happening, but they could not fight it, the king had guards at the door and he was demanding to watch them defile each other.

He watched on quietly guiding them to discover every part of each other's bodies until he disrobed himself and joined the women in the bed. He had his way with both of them and afterwards laughed at the power he exerted. The idea that a guard would defy his rules was near treason. Had the man at the bath house told him it was just a wild fling, he would have just had the girl and punished the boy, but when he was told that Ash had spent a fortune to keep her pure and for himself, then the king felt he had to teach the boy a lesson.

After everything was done the three of them lay in the bed. Ruthie and Wyndsoria had retreated into their selves. They did not recognize that the world was still moving around them. The king lay in between the two proud of himself.

He spoke to the both of them not realizing he was truly speaking to neither of them. "Everyone needs to remember that this is my kingdom. You do not defy my rules. You should not have left the bath house and you should not have second guessed my wishes. You are both mine and no guard will change that no matter who he loves or who his mother is. Now, you shall never be mother and daughter in law." Again, he was proud of his cruel torture of the women and laughed to himself as he got up to speak at the celebration downstairs.

As he put his robes back on he only allowed the women to put on their braziers and undergarments, but nothing more. He felt they needed a little bit of public humiliation to be sure they knew their place.

When Ash and Jaso came over the hill to the sight of Sodorrah, Ash could not get there fast enough. He had to go see Ruthie the first moment he could. Jaso watched as the young boy leaned in and started riding his horse full gallop towards the city.

Everything whipped by Ash in a blur of sensation. The sounds of the winds flying by and the coolness of the fresh air did not faze him as he sped towards his destination. Each step the horse took he was brought a bit more into the life of Sodorrah. The sounds of the market started to come in focus and the scents of the kitchens. Nothing was in Ash's periphery as his entire being was focused on Ruthie.

As he hit the edges of the city he slowed down by necessity, but he did not take any detours, his goal was to get to the bath house as soon as possible. He passed the stadium, the hostels, and the schools. He made a quick turn onto the street with the bath house and dismounted almost before his horse came to a stop. He whipped the reigns around a free standing concrete pillar and stomped into the business.

He swung the door open with excessive force causing paintings and knickknacks to fall off the wall. His armor clanking came to a stop as he was greeted with the scummy smile of the skinny manager.

With a smile on his face Ash announced, "Bring me Ruthie, I have returned."

The little man showed no emotion, just a blank stare on his face. He rubbed his arm in discomfort and slowly walked over to the cash box behind the counter. He took his time, opened it up and started counting money as he continuously looked up trying to keep an eye on the young guard in the entryway of his business.

"What are you doing? I want my woman, I paid for her, I expect you to deliver her." Ash did not know what the man was up to, but he was not pleased.

The man closed the cash box and walked back over to Ash. He handed the boy a large stack of coins. He looked up still stone faced and spoke, "I apologize. Our king came in while you were gone and took Ruthie from our bath house. She is now a concubine to the king. I'm sorry, but it is his will. Here is your money back." He started to hold out the money to put in Ash's hand when he was struck up the side of the head by a metal armored hand.

Coins tossed across the room and the little man crumpled to the floor. He slammed his head against the hard wooden floorboards and barely stayed conscious. The couple people in the room quieted down and shrunk into the corners. The normal response was to look for a magisterial guard, but there was already one present, the attacker.

Ash slowly walked over to the man cowering on the floor. The clanking of his armor chiming like the bells of a funeral dirge. The man looked up fearing for his life begging to be spared and blaming everything on the white king. Ash looked down angry at the man for giving away his love, angry at the king for taking what was his, and angry at God for disrupting his life as he just had.

He knelt down on one knee bringing his face in close to the managers. He reached out with his gauntlet clad hand and grabbed the man's face between his thumb and fingers. "I was going to have to spare you. But, then you blamed our king and savior." The word 'our' was dripping with sarcasm. "That is treasonous. That is punishable by death and I will do my duty as his guard. But, I really want you to know that I will enjoy it because of what you let happen to Ruthie."

The man's eyes widened as he scrambled to get to his feet, but it was in vain as Ash's sword struck straight into his chest. The blunt force of the blow was shocking and broke a couple ribs.

Ash had always imagined stabbing someone would be accompanied by a whooshing sound and a clean cut, but the body gave resistance. The sound of blood gushing out of the wound was accompanied by a thickness in the air. He pushed against the broken ribs, into the internal organs until the sword stumped against the man's spine.

There were some gasps and gurgles, but eventually Ash pulled his sword out of the coming corpse and walked out the door. He didn't feel anything. It did not take his anger away nor did it give him any closure.

He walked out of the bath house and began to mount his horse when Jaso screamed from down the street. "Ash! Stop now!"

Ash let go of the saddle and stepped back waiting for Jaso to approach. He held the bloodied sword to his side and stared down the other guard.

When he got close he dismounted and drew his sword. "Ash, what did you do?"

"I defended our king." He shrugged Jaso off and turned back to his horse. Before he could mount, the back of his helmet was smashed with Jaso's sword handle. He stumbled forward shaking his head trying to refocus from the thud.

Ash kneeling on the ground tightened his grip on his sword and stood up swinging out wide as he spun to face Jaso. Jaso blocked the swing with his own sword, a clang reverberating throughout the street as Jaso screamed at his subordinate, "Your sword is bloodied! You can't just head off from a thing like that." Jaso stepped in swinging his sword down from overhead while Ash blocked it holding his sword sideways with the support of his free hand. "Stand down and explain what happened."

Jaso pulled his sword back and took a step to the left. As Ash stepped right to match Jaso they both swung their swords high. Jaso screamed out, "I said, stand down!" As Ash's eyes followed the swords going up, Jaso hooked Ash's heel with his own foot and swept the kid's balance out from under him. Ash slid sideways as he crashed into the ground hard on his shoulder. The bloody sword fell from his hand and bounced away.

Jaso pointed the tip of his sword at the young man's throat, the weakest point of his armor. He looked into Ash's eyes, "Now, tell me what happened."

Ash without moving a muscle, "I came to see a girl. She was not here. The manager claimed the king took her. He said he stole her, that he kidnapped her. I told him he cannot blame misdoings on our savior. So, I killed him."

Jaso stared into the boy's eyes for a long while until he removed the sword from his throat and held out his hand to help him up. "And, where are you headed now?"

As Ash was pulled up an explosion popped from overhead. Ash smiled looking up at the dissipating reddish cloud, "Back to the palace of course."

Moshe led his small group down out of the new grey land and into the yellow. They did not speak much, but rode their camels in near silence. The cool air was blowing the tall grasses in across the small hills, but they could see the grass giving way to the desert off in the distance.

Mary had tried to keep her camel near Moshe's, but Loht and Buz tended to drift away every so often. They had tried to disappear to convince Moshe to go look for them so they could bring him back to the old fat king's castle, but it had not worked.

Buz had pulled in front of Moshe and stopped his camel creating a slightly captive audience in the new king. "Sire, I must say this is crazy. If we travel all the way to the yellow king's land you most likely die and leave the entire planet alone with no direction."

Mary chimed in feeling this was their only real chance at convincing him this is a mistake, "You need to listen to us. The yellow king is known as the king of violence. You are an amazing leader, believer, and speaker, but you are walking into a death trap. I'm afraid we won't make it to his castle, his citizens may rip you apart when you step foot in the first village."

Moshe curled his brow and thought about what was being said. When Loht and Buz spoke of the dangers he easily ignored them, but he felt it important to listen to what Mary had to say. His heart would not allow him to ignore her.

He tilted his head straight up at the sky above and spoke aloud, "Tell me. You have shown me I need to move on, but you also sent Mary to me and she tells me I need to return. Please lord show me the way." He brought his hands together, looked down and muttered thanks.

When he looked up he saw two lights dancing in front of his eyes. One was bright white while the other was a dark purple. When he focused on the white light he could feel energy pouring into him from all directions. He felt light and happy, but then he turned to the purple light which extended audible cries of pain and a distress in his gut that nearly knocked him off his camel.

The three in his entourage looked on seeing nothing. They just watched as Moshe looked from side to side, smiling at one side grimacing in pain to the other.

Moshe watched the two lights as they leapt up into the air twisting around one another into a brilliant swirl of white and purple. They exploded in the air above and the white light was sent streaming towards the coming desert while the purple retreated back the way they came.

Moshe dismounted his camel and the desert to which they had been driving towards. There he saw light. There were happy faces, the sounds of children playing, and he could feel the embrace of his son. God spoke to Moshe as he looked, "This way is the blood of kings."

Moshe nodded and turned around to face the hills from which they had come and he was faced with darkness and pain. He could see hordes of grey men walking over the hills led by both the yellow and white kings, slaughtering anyone who showed the slightest affiliation to Moshe. He watched Mary as men wrapped a rope around her neck and arms. They pulled them taught so she could not move or breath while more men tore her dress from her body and violated her in ways that turned Moshe's stomach.

Then he saw the white king with Ash by his side. He saw them standing over himself, kneeling on the ground looking up into the eyes of his son clad in the magisterial armor. The king nodded his head and Ash swung his sword down across the neck of Moshe severing the majority of his head. His body slumped to the side with blood pouring from the opened up neck. Ash screamed. The king laughed and turned to walk away. Ash out of terror and sheer regret he fell down at the side of his dying father and cried, screaming his apologies.

The vision faded as God spoke to Moshe again, "This is the way of the forgotten."

Moshe looked over at the three waiting his decision. He showed no apology and said, "God has spoken to me. We move on."

He remounted his camel restarting his journey south. Mary, Loht, and Buz reluctantly followed.

Ash and Jaso allowed their horses to trot back to the palace, watching the spectacle of the explosions overhead as they moved. Ash kept vengeance in his heart, he wanted to return to the castle and murder the king, but it was something he had to think about. If he could only find a way to be alone with the king, he was of the bloodline to overthrow him, maybe this was his destiny.

As the boys made their way up the hill to the immense structure sitting atop it Ash decided that he would begin to look for a time to meet with the king alone as soon as he got back.

The explosions grew louder and louder the higher up the hill they got and when they reached the outer wall the cracking of the signal was nearly ear-shattering.

The two guards crossed the entrance and noticed there was a ball going on. They dismounted and made their way up the steps to the ballroom. When they made it over the top of the stairs and looked down into the room, they were treated with the sight of numerous guards all standing around the outside edge of the party of itself.

They had to push their way through to be able to see the dance floor and the table with the guests of honor. Ash had never seen so many people at one time and never had an inkling that the king's guard force could possibly be so large.

It became apparent to Ash that he would not have a chance to kill the king that night. But, he knew he would lie in wait. He could feel in his bones that he would be the one to oust the king from this world.

While Ash tried to count the guards present at the gala, trumpets blared and the declaration that the king had arrived garnered everyone's attention.

At the top of the stairs appearing from the darkened hallway was the king in his white robes and gaudy crown. But, he had a woman on each arm, scantily clad in what was just enough to cover their breasts and crotches. They are probably just a couple of the concubines from his own personal harem Ash thought. But, as he started to lose interest he recognized the one on the king's right arm as his mother. She leaned in to kiss her king as Ash recognized the woman on the other arm.

It was his beloved Ruthie. The king had not just stolen her away from him, but he had taken her for his own pleasure. The anger returned and Ash wanted nothing more than to rip the king's throat out and stomp on it.

The women disappeared into the darkness from which they came and the king slowly sauntered down the steps. He made his way slowly through the ballroom looking at the faces of each of the guards. He came down the stairs on out onto the dance floor before he spotted Ash.

He walked over to the young boy and stared him straight in the eye and bellowed out, "All guards line up for assignment. It is time I speak with each person who has completed their calling." He smirked as he saw the anger bleed all over Ash's face. As he turned to head to the table of honored guests he raised his right hand and shoed away Ash and the other guards like common houseflies.

Chapter 12

Perceptions

Standing at attention outside the castle was the type of thing Ash had envisioned he would be doing while serving as the king's magisterial guard. But, it shocked him that the first time it happened he would find himself angry at the king. He was ready to kill his representative to God and not regret a moment.

There were thousands of men standing in line with him. After each guard found their captain and learned where they lined up for assignment, they ended up against the outer wall of the palace facing inward awaiting their orders. The sky had become cloudy and the night had overtaken the day. Soon, they would all be shivering in the downpour of rain which the king would avoid and make them wait out there until it had passed. But, as luck would have it the king arrived earlier than most anticipated. He came around the corner flanked by Admiral Devoncote and General Goliath walking very slow with exaggerated straight leg steps. He looked into the eyes of each of his guards as he passed them by.

When he found Ash he stopped his march and faced the

boy. His voice boomed as he began, "You may be walking into certain death." He smirked at Ash then turned and started his walk again. "But, as God chose this path for you, know that this is your destiny. The yellow king is planning an offensive to invade this very city. But, our intelligence has been tipped off and we will not wait for them to invade our sacred land."

There were some cheers and huzzahs from the line of guards. The king nodded and raised his fist in recognition of their loyalty. "We instead will overtake the yellow king and you will be traveling across the sea to Kanan. There you will siege the castle from the south and take the yellow king!"

This emphatic statement was met with a few cheers, but more shock as the last time a king had another killed and removed from the throne was hundreds of years prior. In the light of what they thought of as modern society, it was an unprecedented move.

"You will take the yellow lands in my name," he paused as he walked back over to face Ash, "or you will die trying."

Ash got the message. This wasn't a mission as much as an execution. The yellow king, the violent king, was not a sitting duck for an invasion of a thousand men. He would tear them apart. This was the lengths the king would go to punish a guard who he felt disobeyed his laws.

Ash wanting to give the king the impression he was wrong belted out, "I will happily walk to my death to serve you my lord." Then he knelt on one knee and bowed his head.

As the king walked over to place his hand on the back of Ash's helmet, Ash quietly said a prayer, "God, please give me the strength to accept that which cannot be changed; courage to change that which can be changed."

As he felt the patting of the king's hand on the back of his helmet he heard the deep voice of God fill his head once again, "Child, know that as my chosen defender, you will not die at the hand of another man."

With that Ash rose again and looked the king in the eye, "Thank you sire, I look forward to going on this mission for you."

The king pondered into the eyes of the boy trying to understand if it was all genuine. He came to no conclusion other than he might have to sail the seas himself to witness the death of the disobedient bastard. It also allowed him to avoid having to watch over the boy, just kill the family of the forgotten, that was a much easier plan.

The journey was long and arduous. Moshe and his three companions were exhausted, thirsty, and hungry. The amount of time and sustenance needed was well underestimated. But, they were finally upon the outer most village of the yellow king.

The town was called Braham and, as was the way of most the yellow cities, it was known as a haven of violence. Moshe made sure Loht, Buz, and Mary were aware of the dangers of entering the city and the importance of their anonymity. They approached the village with their faces down and shawls pulled up over their heads.

The transition from desert to city was poignant. As soon as they entered the small town they walked up on a platform that elevated the entire village. There were walls a few feet high randomly placed but it was the walkways that blocked much of the flying sand that plagued most of the desert. It was vastly cleaner and better planned than Listerbourne which was the desert city Moshe had spent most of his life in.

They kept to themselves as they ventured into the town, trying to keep their gazes away from the locals. They reached a small well that was positioned near a church and decided it was their best bet at getting something for their nearly chapped throats.

They dismounted their camels and quietly pulled up the bucket from the well. They took turns getting water. Mary refused the first serving and forced Moshe to take it, but then it went around to her, then Loht, and finally Buz. After Buz took his large gulps the bucket was mostly dry and they dropped it back down the well to retrieve some more.

While the bucket was in transit, a man came out of the church and looked down from the stone steps at the quartet. "Who are you? Taking our water? Invading our town? Who are you?" The man was quickly bouncing down the steps. He had on the robes of a priest, but was not acting in a way that Moshe felt was priestly.

Before he reached the ground he had his dagger drawn and was screaming out for other to hear. "These four are not in peasantry garb, they are not from here. Identify your purpose strangers!"

The sight of the dagger put Loht and Buz into a defensive mode, they both drew their swords and stepped between the two priests. Loht spoke out in an authoritative voice, "We are but travelers, leave us be."

But, the plea was useless, the priest had no intention of letting anyone go free. He motioned to his side as two more men came into view from behind the corner of the church. They were carrying spears and quickly closing in on the group. Moshe turned around to flee in the opposite direction, but saw men closing in from that angle with slingshots and staffs.

The men with the spears lunged towards the group. Buz snapped one of the men's spears with a full swing from his sword and Loht dodged the other using the hilt of his sword to force the spear tip into the ground. Mary exploded from between the two men and sprinted straight at the yellow priest. She connected with a strong thrust of her knee to his groin forcing him to drop his dagger.

Moshe with his back to the action watched his world begin to move in slow motion. As the two men advanced on him he could see a bright light shining at the bottom of the staff of the man on the right. He kicked as hard as he could where the light was shining and the staff spun out of the man's hand and struck him in the throat. The light shot away from the staff man and to the slingshot man who was reaching in his side pouch for ammunition. The light danced on the man's nose which is where Moshe thrusted the palm of his hand. There was a crunching sound and Moshe felt the cartilage bend and snap under the force of his hand.

With all five men on the ground, Moshe removed the shawl he had draped over his head. The staff man who was now gasping for breath looked up and started to squeal. He tried to communicate what he saw, but words did not come out. Mary and the boys were set aback by the sounds, but once the slingshot man looked up through the blood that had detonated across his face he started to grunt and quickly flipped over to where he was on his knees.

Moshe looked down at the man confused, but then heard him call out, "The grey king is here. I'm so sorry sire. Please forgive my mistake." The man was now on both knees with hands pressed together. The blood from his face was spattering across the dirt that neared him. "The grey king is here! Come show your gratitude!" He screamed as he bowed front and back.

The four of them were unsure of what it meant. But, as they looked on in confusion, the other four men all followed suit and got into kneeling positions before their king. As Moshe looked at the blood spattered man he realized it was the cook from the ship. He wanted to reach out to the man and bring him to his feet, but before he could he noticed dozens more people had gathered around them and were kneeling down. Looking down the streets he could see grey men, women and children coming out of doors and looking out windows. Everyone was clamoring to come see the grey king.

Mary turned to Moshe and gave him a strong deep hug. She whispered into his ear giving him chills across his body as her breath whipped past his hair. "You were right my lord. The message has spread here. Speak. Speak to your people."

Moshe turned in a full three hundred sixty degrees. He held his arms out at shoulder height and let the words of God speak through him, "My fellow man. I am here to lead you to freedom. I am here to lead you to a life committed to God and not the kings. I am here to lead you into the castle of the yellow king and take this nation for God!"

The sobs in the concubine quarters were unstoppable. The shear distress of Wyndsoria drained the other women in the room. Genevieve had left the room to avoid the crying while Ruthie was introduced to the concubine quarters, but left after Wyndsoria broke down.

Ruby and the old woman both tried to sooth their fellow concubines sorrows. They held her and rocked her, but her soul was scarred.

Ruby whispered to her, "This is not your fault, you know there is no changing the king's mind once he decides on something."

Wyndsoria replied in a hoarse voice that had been overworked from the sorrow. "I should have said no. I should have refused. How could I betray my son in such a way. How could I damage that girl like that must have done."

The old woman petted Wyndsoria's head, "Child, he would have had you killed if you refused."

"I should be dead! Death would be better than this!" Spittle sprayed from her lips and the tears soaked her face.

Ruby grabbed the woman by her arms and forced her to look her in the face. "You are beautiful and the fact that this is tearing you up proves you are a good person. This is not your fault this is the king, this is his depravity and you can't hold yourself responsible."

"But, what of the girl? This is the type of thing that will drive me mad, but she is just a child."

"Wyndsoria, her calling is that of a prostitute and now a concubine. She has had a tough life, this will not affect her the same way."

The sobs did not slow, she continued to weep beyond her ability to breath. "I should be dead. Everyone would be better off if I had refused and he killed me right then."

Ruby softly spoke, almost reflexively as opposed to out of comfort, "I would not be better off."

Wyndsoria still crying and gasping for breath looked up at the pregnant woman in confusion.

Ruby wrapped her arms around Wyndsoria, "I love you Wyndsoria. Please don't talk about dying. I couldn't bare it."

It wasn't the end of Wyndsoria's tears for the night, but it was a turning point. Everything felt different after that. She continued to weep for what she assumed was the end of any relationship she might have with her son going forward. But, as Ruby held her and comforted her it was no longer just someone who was in a similar situation. She could now feel the love and care the woman had for her and it made the difference that night.

Admiral Devoncote sat on the thinking bench in the garden of the palace. He looked out upon the waterfall of plants that covered a small portion of the outer wall as

Patricka walked up to get her briefing.

Devoncote stood and greeted the girl and waved his hand in front of the bench wanting her to sit for what he had to say. "I have some information for you." He paused. He had enjoyed pushing the girl to mature to the level of her position, but he knew that what he was about to tell her was something that she would have trouble dealing with. If she knew what she should he was about to tell her of a death in the family.

Devoncote looked at the girl and only saw a child. He took a deep breath, ignored the desire to hold her hand and let it out. "We seem to be getting false intelligence from the yellow king. The word out of that kingdom is that there was a coup led by the forgotten against the fat king and he was killed. They have spread across the red and black kingdoms. But, it is just a ploy. They want to us to prepare to battle alongside them so they can catch us unprepared. Our intelligence from the fat kingdom, the red kingdom and the black kingdom is that the forgotten was locked away and rotted." He looked down at the girl who had gone completely pale. "The forgotten has been dealt with."

Patricka did not move, she did not breath. All she could think was her father was dead. Why did Devoncote have to quash her hopes by proving the yellow king's intelligence wrong? She was forced to face reality. She gasped for breath as the world went dark for a moment. She looked back up at the man and asked, "What of the yellow king's story? How did that make it over here?"

"Our spies in each of the other kingdoms stories matched up. Our spy in the yellow kingdom obviously has lost his loyalty to his king. We are dealing with him."

Patricka nodded slowly as she arose from the bench and started to walk away. She gave no inclination that she was done, she just left the meeting.

She did not return to her quarters or the library. She did not know what do or where to go. Her mind replayed story after story of her father playing with her, helping her learn her lessons, and taking care of her when she was hurt. He was gone and she was down to one parent. A parent that would have her forget her father if she could have it her way.

She wandered out of the palace and down the hill. There was nothing that registered with her. The sun had just risen and the market was starting to get going for the day. The smells of meat just starting to cook mixed with the morning dew that was dissipating.

Patricka tried to push her father out of her mind, but he would not leave. She grappled with the idea of how to deal with the pain and loss. She asked herself what adults do.

She turned down a side road and walked into a pub.

The slow back and forth sway of the ocean did not sit well with Ash. He was stuck in a cycle of a growing ache in gut that churned his stomach until he retched over the edge of the ship. Then the cycle would start again.

Unfortunately, the illness did not remove his duty. He was still a guard sent on a mission to invade the yellow king's capital city. He was still a part of the crew that had to sail a ship across the ocean and walk into certain doom.

Ash had just finished his shift of rowing and was now trying to overcome the sickness of the sea. The thick warm air of the ocean forcing salt into his mouth, nose, and eyes, was not helping him reach his goal.

He was one of several hundreds of guards on that particular ship. There was supposed to be a second, but they could not see it following. Ash was convinced they were the only crew of men making the journey.

He knew that the mission seemed impossible, but he

believed in the voice of God that he had heard. Ash would not fall to the hands of another man. He would overthrow the yellow king, not in the name of the white king, but in the name of the people of God.

He slunk down leaning against the railing of the ship, sweat poured out of his face and drool dripped over his lip. Trying to get a grip on his equilibrium another man walked up to him.

The man looked about as pathetic as Ash, with sweat and spit pouring from his face. "It is better when you heave. Just let it loose into the ocean and you'll feel better for a few minutes." The man was not a convincing posterchild for the method.

"Thanks. But, nothing seems to help." Ash responded.

The man sat down next to Ash leaning his head against the rails. "This isn't how I hoped to serve in the guard. I get to travel across the sea, sick as a dog just to arrive and be slaughtered by the violent king."

Ash cocked his head at his new conversation companion.

"Look, I know I am supposed to sing the praises of our king, but I'm going to die anyway. I thought if I insulted the king you might do me a favor and kill me right here."

Ash tried to laugh, but the contraction of his stomach muscles nearly brought on another bout of vomiting. He took a deep breath and spoke more freely to the man, "I understand. We have been committing ourselves to lives of slavery. We have been following the kings as if they were God and ignoring our own God in the process."

The man closed his eyes both to ponder what Ash was saying and an attempt to sooth his nausea. "I thought I was being bold and treasonous."

"Think about it." Ash was starting to feel the passion behind what he was saying. "We are going out here to die.

We have no plan and no leader and no hope of survival. Then why don't we at least spend the last days of our lives fighting for ourselves. Let's go in planning on overthrowing the yellow king and taking his land and living free."

The man nodded in agreement. He wanted to stand in unity with Ash, but his queasy belly would not allow him to become quite so upright. "You know, you are right. We should have marched against the kings long ago."

The two men sat against the rail praying to puke. They prayed the journey across the ocean was almost over. They prayed they could overtake the yellow king. They prayed they could be free. They prayed for survival.

Braham had treated Moshe and his group quite well. But, their stay was coming to an end, they could not continue to rally the troops without a plan of attack. Moshe stood in front of the church talking about God and their mission. He spoke of freedom and why it was necessary to overthrow the kings.

He spoke to his people with the authoritative voice he had come to adopt. "Just as we have spread the message of freedom for the grey skinned to the villages surrounding the yellow king we must spread the message to the castle itself. We must infiltrate the walls and speak to the king's inner circle."

There was a discomfort that spread through the air of the church. The people of Braham did not want to interrupt their leader, but there was something that he did not understand.

"We have spread this message into the kingdom of the fat king, who is no more. We have spread this message into the kingdoms of the red and black kings who are on the defensive. Now we overthrow the yellow king with our ideas instead of his violence."

Murmurs started within the pews of the church. One of the native greys of the yellow kingdom stood up. "I'm sorry sire. I don't mean to interrupt." The young man said in a meek tone that almost allowed him to hide behind the wispy voice. "But, the city of Kanan is not an open city. No one from the kingdom is allowed there unless requested by the king himself."

The man sat down to a large sound of mumbles that bounced around the room. The idea that their leader was not prepared for this worried much of the congregation.

Moshe looked up to the roof of the church and spread his arms ready to take in the warmth and knowledge of God. And, although he heard nothing and no lights came dancing before his eyes, he could see something in the wood of the ceiling above. Within the natural lines of the woodgrain he could make out a word, "Siege."

He turned his attention back to the congregation. "If we cannot overtake the king with peace, then we must lay siege on his castle. Go! Spread out and deliver the word that tomorrow night we approach the city of Kanan and on my signal we storm the castle."

He could feel the nervousness of the people. "There are times in history when men must stand up for their future and this is one of those times. Although, you have lived your lives in fear of your kings you will now stand up in unity and tear down their powers. Go! Go to the east to deliver the news to the people of Gamom who already stand for our freedom and tell them tomorrow we siege! Go! Go to the west to deliver the news to the people of Bylon who already stand for our freedom and tell them tomorrow we siege! Go to all the villages of this great land and tell them tomorrow we take back our nation for us and for our God!"

The speech was not met with cheers, but all the citizens

understood what was at stake. They left with purpose and a mission. As the last few people filed out of the church Mary stayed behind to watch Moshe in his post sermon ritual. He always stayed back and relived what the room did as he replayed his speech in his head.

After he had heard the entire thing he dropped his head in worry. He felt there was no chance. He did not build enough desire in his followers. Mary came up to the altar and stood behind him, she wrapped her arms around his waist and laid her head on his back.

Moshe croaked out, "It is certain death."

"Maybe." She responded not trying to sugar coat the situation. "But do you think God is leading us to our demise?"

He shook his head understanding her point. She gently turned him around to face her and she grabbed him by the back of his neck and pulled him in for a deep long kiss. She was starting to let tears flow. "Moshe, I love you. I want you. I want to be with you forever. But, I am afraid this may be our last days on this planet."

He looked down at her scared and saddened face, "I love you too. But, I am married."

She slapped him turning her tone to something much more strict. "You are still showing your loyalty to that bastard white king! You are not married in the eyes of God and you know it. Stop being blinded by your history and commit to your God." She kissed him again, only harder and with more urgency. "If you don't then tomorrow we will all be dead."

Moshe heard something that he should have heard when God spoke to him, but it took the woman who meant more to him than his own life did. Wyndsoria was his past. Mary was his future. God and the kingdom of the greys was the future.

He took Mary by the hand and led her to the center of

the church. He pulled the ceremonial ribbon from the trim of his robes. "Mary, I love you and if God will have it I commit myself to you. I pledge to be one entity with you for now and for all of eternity."

Mary held a finger up to his lips and whispered while dreaming through his eyes, "Please, if we are going to be with one another don't call me Mary. Please, call me Maggie."

He held his palm up to Mary Maggie and she held hers against his. He used his other hand to wrap the ribbon around their hands and bind them together as one. He held up his other palm and she pressed her other hand against his. He spoke in ritual, "Although we are two separate people, God has bound us together as man and wife for eternity. As my left hand is your right we shall never be separated in the eyes of God. As my right hand is not your left, but God binds us we can never separate for any great distance. This is our solemn connection and our pledge to each other and our God. There is none other here, but Moshe, Maggie, and God himself."

He pulled his right hand away from hers and wrapped his arm around her waist. He pulled her in and pressed his body against hers while they fell into a deep kiss that washed away the world.

The joy of their never ending life together mixed with the fear that their lives and world was about to end pushed them to a desperate attempt to steal that moment and let it live forever. Alone in the church Moshe and Mary Maggie created their everlasting life. Naked and in front of the eyes of God they made love and allowed that moment to live forever.

Chapter 13

Connections

Vomiting over the side of the ship did not cease as the journey went on. Ash found himself with a drastic lack of sleep as each time he drifted off it was only minutes before his body jolted him awake with the desperate need to heave over the railing. There wasn't anything left for him to turn out, but the desperation of the act stuck around.

The night had fallen and the ship continued to sail on. The mood on the ship dropped as the realization that there was no real plan and very little hope swept over each of the passengers. They continued to serve their shift in the rowing rooms and they ate their meals, but the feeling of impending doom loomed closely.

Ash laid on the hard wet wood of the upper deck. The sound of the oars hitting the water in a specific rotation mixed the snap of the sails as the wind came and went. He looked up at the night sky and wondered what would happen once they landed.

His mind tried to answer the question. He came up with scenarios such as the yellow king waiting for them on shore and they would be killed off before their feet would ever touch land again. He thought of the idea that there may be outer villages in the south that blocked their ability to reach the king. But, as these terrible outcomes came to Ash, a deep voice filled the air once again, "You will not die at the hand of another man."

Ash sat up teasing his stomach with the sudden movement allowing the queasy feeling to radiate throughout his body. Breathing slowly to calm the nausea he looked up to the sky and asked, "Then, tell me what to do. I can't go into an invasion blind." Before the words left his lips the sky began to light up. The stars twirled and soared through the blackness creating a scene for Ash.

Stars left their position and created a cluster that resembled a castle. And more stars lined up below the castle, waving back and forth looking like the shoreline. A star above the castle began to pulse very slowly. He watched the shoreline wave and the castle stand tall when he noticed the pulsing begin to quicken.

As the pulsing star sped up its tempo another group of stars came in from the bottom. They crossed the shore line and slowly spread out around the southern, eastern, and western sides of the castle. The pulsing star lit up brighter than any other star in the sky and the groups of stars instantly swarmed the castle.

The sky went dark again and all the stars returned to their normal position. Ash nodded his head and was about to thank God for his direction when he heard a cough come from behind him. He slowly turned around got to his feet to see a group of ten men all staring at the sky.

One of the men in the group spoke with a voice that felt like death itself, "It is a timer to our deaths." He pointed out at the sky to the star which was still pulsating at a very slow rate.

Ash grabbed the railing of the ship to keep his dizziness form toppling him over. "It is not a timer for our deaths. It is a sign from God to count down to our destiny!" He paused to gauge the response. The men seemed to be understanding and getting behind him. He pushed the sickness back into his stomach. "The king was sending us to certain death, but God has another plan! That…" Ash turned to face the star that was pulsating and nearly vomited from the equilibrium change. "That is a sign from God himself. That is the countdown to us doing something for ourselves instead of our king."

The man who spoke before, stepped forward, "What do we have to lose?" He gave Ash a hard pat on the back forcing him to rush to the railing to be sick again.

Moshe stood outside the church looking at the glorious wonders of the Earth. He looked out over the edge of the city wall and out into the desert. It wasn't his home, it wasn't the place he lived all his life, but it was the same. He could picture the sight of Listerbourne. He peered out into the flat empty land lit only by the light of the moon and he could imagine the small huts of his friends and family. He could see Wyndsoria playing with Patricka. He could smell the meats drifting from the center of town and hear his son asking for advice.

He didn't miss his old life. It was a chance for him to say goodbye to it. Behind him in Braham Maggie slept. She was his future if there was to be a future. He didn't know where they would end up, but he knew that if he survived the siege he would return to her.

He looked up at the stars for advice from God. It was the last time that he would ask for help from the divine and receive it.

He looked up into the sky and spoke aloud, "Please, lord. I need some guidance. I want to give in. I want to go home, but it is for my love of you, my love for my former family, and my love for Maggie that I keep pushing forward. I need to understand what is going to happen. Tomorrow we leave for the castle. I don't know when to attack. I don't know how to attack." He would have continued on rambling about how lost he was, but the stars lit up for him as they had so many times before and as they never would again.

The stars swirled in a great vision and then clustered to show Moshe the same landscape his son was looking at. He could see the stars forming the castle, a line of stars waving in the night showing the southern shore. The vision for Moshe showed a group of stars coming down from the north and forcing their way into the castle. As they started to break through he could see the other stars coming in from the south. And he also saw the pulsating star that exploded with light when all the stars converged on the constellation palace.

Everything went dark and the one star began to pulse very slowly. Moshe looked up and asked, "Is that my signal? I should lead my men when the star illuminates?"

The world swept away in Moshe's eyes. He was left standing in a timeless void feeling the love of God deep within his soul. The voice of God spoke to him for the last time, it filled his ears, his body, and his essence. "Moshe. You have served me well. I want you to understand that. Your destiny is served tomorrow and your place in my kingdom has been reserved. There are still two endings that could come to pass. In one you will serve as a beacon for all mankind for years to come. In the other your life will become a legend that will break hearts for centuries. But, I have recognized your faith and loyalty, your marriage to Mary, and the sacrifices you have made."

With that God's voice left Moshe's life forever, but the

love of God now lived within him.

The door to the concubine's quarters opened quietly in the middle of the night. All five girls were sleeping in their individual beds. A guard walked in clanging his armor, but not violently enough to wake anyone. He came over to Wyndsoria. He shook her shoulder and awoke her.

The sight of the large man encased in silver startled her, but she knew what he wanted.

"The king requires your presence." He whispered unnecessarily.

She nodded and sat up in her bed. She waved her fingertips at the man shooing him away so she could get dressed. The guard obliged and waited at the door for her.

Wyndsoria had been dreading this meeting with the king. The last two encounters with him had left distraught and nearly suicidal. She was not sure if she could manage to lower herself to his desires. She put on a brazier, blouse, undergarments, skirt, and shoes as slowly as she could possibly manage. But, in the end she dressed herself and walked hunch-shouldered to the door for her escort to take her to her burden.

Walking down the hallways she peeked in on doors that were cracked open and witnessed some of the other jobs in the castle. She saw a poet, a juggler, a cook, a cleaner, and a musician. She imagined how simple things would be if she had been assigned one of those callings. If her only worry was to be sure the castle was clean or that all the events had appropriate music written, she would not be faced with the torments as such she was about to endure.

The fantasy she was playing in her head dissolved as they reached the king's chambers. The door was opened for her and she walked in to see the king laying in his bed naked, fully exposing his disgusting vulnerabilities to her.

"Disrobe slowly. I want to savor it." The king had the same lecherous tone in his voice that had been there the last two meetings Wyndsoria had with him. She shuddered at the command, but did her best to comply.

She unbuttoned her blouse feeling the degradation of what was to come with every button. She pulled it down off her shoulders exposing the skin and humiliation of not controlling her own body. And, as she unsnapped and began to remove her brazier the tears came. She pushed her emotions down attempting to swallow her sense of self, but it could not stop the sobbing.

The king, frustrated with the girl, stood up and yanked her skirt and knickers down to the ground. He grasped her forearms with great strength causing immediate bruising to form. He swung to the side forcing her momentum towards the bed where she fell face first.

"I don't understand your crying. You are my concubine. You do what I want. You are mine and I want you right now. Why are you crying?"

She tried to get it out. She tried to tell him, but her words were not coherent as she panicked while the man came behind and pushed her into the bed while he carried out what he planned to do. "You were… hate… Ruby… Ash and Ruthie…" They were just parts of sentences.

Her sobbing intensified as she gasped for breath with her face being pushed into the sheets. She could feel his violations to her being from the inside and out. She cried and prayed for it to end.

The king let off the pressure on her head as he flipped her over onto her back. As soon as she saw his face she blurted out, "Evil bastard."

This caught him off guard. He stopped his movements and got off her. Looking down she could see the anger building in his face. He grabbed her by the hair and drug her off the bed. "Evil bastard? I am your savior! I am your king, your lover, and your God!" Once she got to her feet he flung his fist full of her hair to the side smashing her face against the stone wall.

Her nose snapped splattering blood across the grey stones. The force of the blow instantly caused the left half of her face to throb in pain. He pulled his hand back forcing her to look him in the eye. "Genevieve told me you had no loyalty, but I just assumed it was concubine jealousy. I was wrong. She said you and Ruby were both disloyal. Talking bad about your king. Was she right about that as well?"

Wyndsoria did not respond only blew bubbles as she tried to breathe through the river of blood pouring from her nose. After a couple seconds of silence, he slammed her face back into the wall shredding the skin against the grainy rock. Blood poured into Wyndsoria's right eye as she was face to face with the king again. He spat in her face and pushed her to the ground. He quickly put his robes on and grabbed her by the hair again. He pulled her to the door and kicked it open.

The guards on the other side jumped in shock and turned to help their king. The king shoved the girl to one of the armored men and shouted, "Drag her useless body and follow me."

Each of the guards grabbed one arm and started walked at a very fast pace. Wyndsoria's knees were dragging on the ground, slamming against the cracks and divots in the rock. She started to get her footing to walk with the group when the king turned around and kicked her in the shin, knocking her back to the ground. "I said drag her don't escort her."

The rest of the way she did not fight it. She hung there lifeless wondering if her shin had been broken and trying to blink the blood out of her eye.

When they arrived at the concubine's quarters the king opened the door with a vengeance causing such a crash that all the girls popped up in their beds. Genevieve's smile shone so bright when she realized what had happened, it almost lit up the room.

The king pointed at the bloodied woman dangling from the guards grasps and screamed, "This is a treasonous wench! She does not know her place or purpose as my concubine. I am going to take her and make her watch me slice apart her son and daughter before I let my sword have some fun with her."

Ruby was shaking her head and whispered out, "No!" But, she whispered it a bit too loud.

The king heard it and pointed at the pregnant girl. "Take her too and lock them up on the Expansion. And grab the whore as well."

One guard dropped Wyndsoria who could no longer support herself. She smashed her face on the ground as the guard charged across the room to apprehend Ruby.

Patricka spent a long time at the pub. She tried a variety of drinks and eventually settled on a stream of rum drinks sweetened with different non-liquor beverages. Being as small as she was and as unaccustomed to alcohol as she was it did not take a lot of them to bring her to the point of a drunken stupor.

After three drinks her words started to slur and everything became very funny to her. The bartender tried to cut her off mostly out of annoyance, but she pulled out her magisterial scarf to show everyone there that she was an important person. The bartender did not want to deal with denying a member of the magisterial court anything. If they decided to hold a grudge many unfortunate events could result for the business.

Instead the barkeep kept the drinks coming. He tried to make small talk with the girl. He questioned how such a young girl was working for the king. He asked why she was drinking so early in the morning. But, everything was met with drunken slurs, shoving her scarf in his face and demands for more drinks.

She stayed there for hours. The day turned to lunch time and eventually into dinner time. As the sun was going down she had woken up from being passed out for the third time that day.

A group of rowdy young men came into the pub high fiving and making crude jokes. They were excited for a fun night after a full day of working maintenance on the castle. They ordered their drinks and shrank away to a corner of the bar.

Patricka stayed on her stool with a full drink in front of her. The world was spinning and flashing to the point that she couldn't possibly take another drink. She tried continue through the disorientation, but instead she passed out on the bar counter.

When she awoke the world was spinning less, but she was still drunk. The boys had moved close by, just a few stools down the bar from her. They were getting louder and sliding drinks between each other on the bar-top. As Patricka put her head back down on the counter one of the drinks came sliding down the bar and slammed into the side of her head.

The startling impact knocked her off her stool. The boys broke out in immediate laughter.

She was not pleased and even though she couldn't see straight she got to her feet and stumbled over to the boys.

She shoved the closest one and mumbled some nonsensical utterance. She tried to stare him down, but her head moved slowly in a small circle with one eye opened wider than the other. The boy stood up ready to teach the girl a lesson. When she reached out to slap him the boy pushed her down and then pulled out a small knife from his boot. He had a sinister smile on his face with obviously ill-intentioned ideas on his mind.

When Patricka got back to her feet and saw the knife, she pulled out her magisterial scarf and tossed it at the boy with the knife. Seeing the scarf froze all the boys at once. The idea that they could be threatening someone from the king's court made their lives flash before their eyes.

Patricka reached out and took the knife from the boy. She slowly walked around him while he stood stone still holding his palms up in full view. She waggled the knife pretending to cut a person and giggled at the ridiculousness. Each step, as she circled the boy, was slightly askew and the bartender thought she would stumble at any moment and who knew who would be blamed for her injuries at that point.

She turned quickly to face the boy and held the knife inches away from his throat. Suddenly appearing much more sober than expected she spoke quietly yet very stern, "I was thinking I should slit your throat just to experience it. If you were going to pick on a little girl you deserve it anyway."

She dropped the knife and broke out in tremendous laughter. She buckled over kneeling on the floor, hands flat against the dusty stone trying to keep herself from falling on her face from a mixture of the alcohol and laughter.

Eventually, she got back to her feet and left the bar allowing everyone to finally be able to relax. Patricka stumbled out of the pub and down the street laughing at the sky calling out to her dead father. "Dad, why did you have to be a prophecy? Why did you have to die? Why do we have to live this way?" Suddenly a club hit her on the back of the head and she crumbled to the ground.

She was scooped up by the guard who clubbed her and took her to the magisterial ship the Expansion.

The land peaked over the edge of the ocean's horizon. Ash felt his stomach drop as the sight was recognized by his brain. All the fear and questions he had about the ability to survive and succeed in overthrowing the yellow king all hit him at once.

He started to wonder if maybe he had the wrong strategy. Maybe the entirety of the ship could pledge allegiance to the yellow king and live in his land serving him. But, the idea of pledging allegiance to the violent king when he had heard the voice of God command him to go forth with his mission was an insane plan. He felt that both God and the yellow king were too vengeful for that plan to be successful.

"Land ho!" He screamed out knowing that he needed to alert the rest of the crew. He looked up into the sky of the midday sun. The pulsating star was still visible, but had not sped up.

Some of the crew came up to the top deck where Ash had screamed out. It was an oddly inspiring sight. They reached the deck holding up their hands to shield their eyes from the painful sunshine. But looking out they saw a lonely man, Ash, leaning against the rail of the ship with the faintest hint of land showing in the background. His pensive look was in stark contrast to the pained, sick, and worried visage he had been donning for the last few days.

The men who had been acting as navigators looked out on the boy seeing hope. They saw the weight of mankind on his shoulders, but the shimmering of the sun on the water illuminating his face told them that he was not only going to stand tall for all of them, he was protected by the light of God and progress of destiny.

Ash turned to face the group of men and holding in his nausea, as he had been learning to do over the last few hours, he repeated in a less forceful tone, "Land ho."

One of the men asked, "Should we prepare to land?"

Ash pointed up at the star that pulsated in the daylight. "When that speeds up we land, right now we hold off."

Moshe halted his troops as they began to see the yellow king's castle in the distance. He asked Loht and Buz to spread the word that this would be camp until the time came to siege.

The mood of the makeshift army was positive. They seemed to be able to focus on living life as opposed to the bloody slaughter that was likely to come. Mothers sat and fed their children. The older children role played the coming battle. The men prepared their weapons and armor. It felt like a normal village, but without the houses and markets that made modern society what it was.

Moshe and Maggie sat at the southernmost point of their camp keeping an eye on the castle. Just in case someone approached from it they wanted to be aware. As the day drove on the other cities in the area joined their camp. There were groups of grey families from the east, west, and north that made the journey to stand up to their king.

In the end there were thousands of men, women and children that were willing to give up their life and their home to attempt to be free and serve their God as opposed to their king.

As the night started to take over the day, Moshe found a stone to stand upon to speak to this army of God. "Thank you! Thank you for coming and making our world a better place." He paused as the crowd quieted down. "I speak to you as the grey king. Not someone to oversee you, not someone to control you, but someone who has heard the voice of God and wants to communicate it to you."

"I don't know when we will move out. That is also up to God. He has given us a beacon. A signal in the sky. As it speeds up we approach the castle and when it glows a bright hot white in the sky we will attack."

Cheers from the crowd erupted. "But, please know this is not vengeance. This is a command from God himself to take his land back from the kings. This is God telling us to be our own people and serve him by putting aside what the king has said and wanted."

"God has told me we are not alone. We have taken the land of the fat king. We have almost overthrown the red and black kings. Right now we focus on the yellow king. There will be other armies God is sending to help us. So, focus on the mission. Do not betray your fellow man. If a man loves God then he shall live. If a man denounces God by devoting himself to the king then he shall die." He paused again to breathe through the discomfort of speaking about murder. "We charge on the signal and we attack due south, in through the front gate."

The families hugged and cheered at the moment they all knew was coming, but all Moshe could see was hundreds if not thousands of people who were crying their last tears and cheering their last cheers.

Chapter 14

Action

God quickened the pace of the star's pulses. The signal caught the eye of Ash almost immediately. He was screaming down deck to the crew that it was time to change course and head inland. The sails fell, catching the wind with a loud popping sound.

In almost no time the direction of the ship was turned and it was heading straight inland. As each minute passed by they could make out the shoreline better and better. With each crashing wave that swept past the huge ship the night fell darker and darker.

Ash did not know how long they had until they would need to be attacking, but he knew as long as they were heading towards land they were moving in the right direction.

Luckily the sickness had mostly dried up within him and he could focus on the tasks at hand. He ran down the stairs and into the rowing room. He got to the front of the room and held his hands to his mouth for a makeshift megaphone. "We are approaching the shore now. Prepare to invade the yellow king's palace. When we hit land we will break into three groups. The first group will storm the castle head on, the other two will flank the sides."

Through all the heaving and grunting of the men rowing the ship, they grasped the idea as well as the importance of their mission. They kept their focus on their chore, but nodded their understanding to Ash.

Ash leapt across the room and went down another deck to make the same announcement for those who were taking a quick nap. He sprinted up and down the ships decks making sure everyone was informed. After he was comfortable with the crew's knowledge he headed back up to the top deck and looked out over the railing.

It was an ominous sight. The night had fully covered the blue of day, but the bright pulse of the signal star lit up much of the shoreline. The waves crashed on themselves as they drew closer to shore. An inky black look took over the ocean as the darkness allowed no other interpretation of the water. Off in the distance the shoreline could be seen becoming deeper and shorter as the tide swelled up and down. Rising up from the darkened shore with the black waters stood a monument to the power of the kings, fortress for the violent king.

It seemed to almost rise up directly from the sea. There was a huge wall that surrounded what appeared to be a half dozen spires. Each spire was a straight cylinder with a pointed top that was reminiscent of a candle flame. The moon and signal star shined down bright on the spire tops and reflected their gold composition back at Ash.

He was mesmerized by the huge structure and couldn't take his eyes away when the ship ran into ground causing a violent stopping of the large vehicle. Although they were still hundreds of yards away from the area of shore they could walk in, the humongous ship was too big to get so close to shore.

With having run aground the crew began to pour out of the lower decks with a mission scrawled across their faces. Ash turned to see the horde of grey men rushing across the wooden deck with hatred in their eyes. What a few days before was a group of men who had resigned to being put to death was now a group of men who had something to live for, something to kill for. The few times Ash spent talking to people about a possible chance at freedom had multiplied into hundreds of small conversations about the boy who controlled the stars. He watched them leap up onto the railing and dive the seemingly endless drop to the black ocean below. It felt like the rampant charge of men would never cease, but after a while the flow slowed. Ash looked out over the edge of the ship and witnessed hundreds of men swimming to shore looking like a swarm of dolphins splashing their way towards land.

Ash looked up at the pulsing star which was constantly glowing brighter and he nodded at his mission. He stood up on the railing and took a deep breath before diving off into the void of the ocean.

Patricka had not awoken since she was thrown into the lower deck of the Magisterial Ship Expansion. Wyndsoria occasionally checked on her to make sure she was still breathing, but everything seemed fine. She did not try and awake the girl, she just wanted her to sleep and dream of a happier place than where they were.

The room was dark, the only light let in was from the moonlight that fed through the spaces in the boards of the deck above. The ocean crashed around them and the room tilted and swirled in too many directions.

Ruthie was asleep in the corner, huddled into a little ball trying to keep warm. Wyndsoria sat leaning against a wall holding Ruby's head in her lap trying to keep the woman calm. She had been having pains in her stomach and was worried about the child growing within her. There wasn't much that could be done, just comfort and care.

The room they were in was large and had comforts held within it, but in the dark of night and awaking from their violent abduction the only comfort they had been able to find was a bucket of water and a rag. It had come into good use as Wyndsoria tried to use it to keep her wounds clean.

Her eye was mostly swollen shut and almost got lost in connection with her now oversized nose. The blood from the open wounds had crusted up on her face and kept her from showing too much emotion as any big facial movement was accompanied by cracking and burning of the skin.

The fear of where they were going or what was going to happen was so intense her mind pushed it away. She had heard the king say he was going to kill her and her family, but her brain rejected it. She felt clueless in their journey and wanted to focus her efforts on mothering the other three women in the room.

With the two younger girls out she could focus on Ruby. She shushed her moans and stroked her hair. Humming sweet songs and telling her it would be ok was a sort of bliss for her at that moment. It allowed her to feel needed and gave her a purpose beyond being the king's personal cargo. If she could have lived forever in that feeling as the person Ruby needed most in the world she would have. But, the waving of the ship and white noise of the sea brought slumber to Wyndsoria.

Moshe and Maggie had stayed near the front of the encampment enjoying each other's company and watching the families live their lives in as much of normality as they could. The night had fallen and much of the army had retired to their makeshift tents.

Maggie leaned in to Moshe, gave him a kiss on the cheek and pointed to the sky. Moshe looked up and saw the signal star blinking at a rapid pace. The sight made his heart pound in his chest and his breath escaped him as the fearful act he had been preparing for suddenly arrived. He no longer had time to convince himself that he could achieve his goal, he could no longer build himself up. He was out of time.

He struggled to get to his feet to alert the army. Many of the men had already noticed and were putting on their animal skins, grabbing their weapons, and preparing for battle. As the group followed their individual rituals to prepare for true sacrifice Moshe stood up on a nearby rock, "The time is now! Do not be afraid. We siege on the castle. Heading due south we will infiltrate the castle from the main gate. Only fight those who resist as all men are our brethren. God is sending other armies to assist so do not attack unless they are hostile."

This did not feel like the mobs of people who listened to him in the fat kingdom. There was something different this time. He did not know that anyone listened to him, but he hoped they did.

Moshe looked to the sky and asked God if he was doing the right thing. There was no answer. He raised his hands to the sky and screamed out, "Please, lord, tell me I am on the right path." The only sounds he heard were those of the swords running across rocks and shields banging together. He looked up at the stars and only saw the signal star flashing quickly.

He realized what felt like it was missing. He felt that God was missing. For the first time in his life he felt that God had left him alone. But, before he could second guess his mission, Maggie grabbed his hand. She leaned in close to him and whispered, "It's time to go." As the breath of her words hit his ear he felt the comfort again. The comfort he had reserved for God was now fulfilled by Maggie.

His confidence surged back into his body and he screamed out, "Siege!" He leapt off the rock and grabbed his staff as he started running towards the castle. The entirety of the camp followed suit. Thousands of men, women, and children flew through the desert landscape under the light of the bright signal star. Random cheers and screams were spread out into the flatness of the terrain.

Moshe did not lead the charge for long, he was not one of the most fit in the army of the greys. He was quickly passed by young strong men that led the way to the castle.

The sand of the yellow kingdom flew up and dirtied the faces of those who weren't in the front of the charge. They could see the castle building in size as they continued their advance. The size of the monument should have been a discouraging force to the army, but as they approached their anger swelled.

In the last few minutes of running towards the building there was no sign that the yellow king expected their approach. The castle remained silent and no lights erupted from any of the windows. It just sat there unchanging.

There was an explosion overhead. The signal had erupted into a glorious cloud of reds, blues, and greens. The light from the explosion lit up the land as if it were daylight.

The younger of the men reached the castle which on its north face housed a huge wooden door split down the center with hinges on both edges. The men initially slammed their bodies into the thick wood and there was no response from the door. It did not budge. They drew their swords and began to hack at the wood. Those who did not have swords kicked at the door, but nothing made a dent.

As the group grew larger with more and more of them

reaching the castle, guards from within began to appear at the tops of the outer wall. Moshe had got close enough to see what was approaching, but there was nothing he could do. No scream would be loud enough and no warning would have been earlier enough.

Moshe watched from a distance as the guards from inside leaned over the edge of the wall and began to rain down arrows on the nearly defenseless below. The screams began immediately as the arrows sliced through the men with no discrimination. Blood exploded from bodies as arrows cut through arms and legs. One man caught an arrow in the neck while another looked up at the wrong time to see an arrow as it pierced his eye and into his skull.

Moshe fell to his knees as he saw the carnage. The army flowed past him still charging the castle. Maggie caught up to him and tried to get him to stand, but the sight of his fellow man using the corpses of their fallen friends as shields from the arrow storm above destroyed his spirit.

He pushed himself and got to his feet just in time to see the guards at the top of the wall lifting cauldrons of molten steel. He fell back to his knees staring at the ground as he heard the sizzling screams of men as their skin burned off their bodies.

"I can't watch. This was a mistake." Moshe had tears flowing down his face. Maggie reached down and wrapped her arms around the kneeling man. The touch of his wife again renewed his spirits. It brought his sense of purpose back and he returned to his feet.

When Moshe began marching towards the castle again he could see the door in the outer wall had caught fire from the falling molten steel and was splitting into humongous chunks, falling onto the men below, but also the flames reached up past the heights of the wall and burned some of the guards.

As he made his way towards the battle there were men pulling weapons from the burned and shredded bodies around them, guards shooting arrows and dumping stones over the edge of the wall with the occasional guard falling to his death. The sounds were horrendous and only topped by the increasingly thick scent of battle.

Moshe was just a few strides away from the wall when the doors cracked and fell open throwing embers in all directions, blinding men with flaming ash that destroyed their retinas.

Moshe kept walking. He stepped through the bonfire of a door with embers and flames flying around his body. As he entered through the outer wall much of his army came streaming in behind him, passing him as they spread out in their invasion of the castle. There was no doubt in Moshe's mind where to go, he was headed for the king and with the egos of royalty he must be in the tallest spire in the palace.

He walked forward with a purpose. The world continued around him, but he did not participate. Men fighting for their lives in every direction, the sounds of metal slicing flesh alongside the stampedes of panic. Moshe focused beyond the world he was in and saw the central tower. He stomped towards it seeing the open archway that would lead to his destiny.

Within feet of entering the arch a large blunt force slammed into Moshe's shoulder. He lost his balance and went flailing to the dirt floor. To his right stood a short, but wide man with steel gauntlets on his arms swaying back and forth preparing for Moshe to retaliate.

Moshe slowly stood up using his staff as a support tool. "We are here to liberate the people of this planet from the kings who circumvent our God. Do you stand with God or the heathens?" Moshe's voice had an authoritative ring to it as he went into his hellfire and brimstone sermon voice.

The little big man shook his head, "I spit on your God. I live for my king and…" There were no more words, just a thick wooden staff striking the jaw of man.

Teeth hit the dirt and the man's jaw waggled in an unnatural way. The man lost his passion for his king as a tirade of gut wrenching squealing screams came from the now deformed face. Moshe wiped the blood off the end of his staff and walked back to the archway.

He walked through the entry of the spire. There was a main room at the bottom that housed weapons of many sorts. He walked across the room and looked over the many implements of torture that set cradled in a wooden rack. He passed over the spears, the swords, the daggers, the hammers, and hatchets. His hand found the handle of a barbed mace. He grasped the strong wooden handle and let the four-pound steel ball hang from its chain. As he walked out of the room to the stairs that wrapped the outer edge of the building he could feel the steel shaving of the ball catch his clothes as it bounced from his gait.

He walked up the stairs with a slow and steady purpose. His mind was awash of morality and he was instead on a mission from God. He was entranced with the anger of his God and was set to destroy the blasphemers.

As he ascended the stairs he could feel his purpose growing and his destiny approaching. He passed a window and upon looking out over the palace he could see another army of men coming in through the southern edge of the city. The wall had crumbled and men were stampeding through the gap in the structure. Looking out he could see that men were swimming in from a ship out in the ocean. Under the daylight of the exploded star it looked like an endless swarm of attackers just as his own army had appeared.

He continued his entranced walk up the stairs. The recognition of the additional armies attacking the castle confirmed the messages he had received in the stars. There was no stopping now.

Nearly half way up the spire he came across a door. He kicked it open creating a slam that shook the walls. Nothing was inside, just a pile of cleaning equipment. He returned the stairs.

A few more steps up and a flaming cannonball came bounding down the stairs echoing a deep metal clang as it hit each stone step. It was covered in tar and leaving a trail of burning stickiness in its wake. Moshe had to leap against the inner wall to avoid the adhesive fire. Returning to his ascent he began to jump two steps at a time to reach the dispenser of the cannonball.

A few more steps up and another cannonball came scorching down the stairs. This one crashed into Moshe's thigh nearly snapping his femur. It burned instantly through his robes and attached the fire directly to his skin.

He screamed out in a pain that stifled his divine mission. Suddenly, stopping the pain became more important than fulfilling destiny.

Dropping to the stairs he scraped his thigh against one of the stone steps starting near the knee and lowering his body against the sharp rock. The pain of his skin tearing off his flesh was excruciating, but the flames dwindled into embers. He moved up two steps and scraped his leg against another step, this time from the top down. Again, his skin gave way to the burning glue sticking to the stone.

Moshe stumbled to his feet looking down at the bloody carnage he had left behind as another cannonball came thudding down the stairs. He jumped to the side just in time to miss what could have been his demise.

A few more stairs up and Moshe came face to face with the cannon-ballers. Inside a room on a small landing on the way up they were each holding the edge of a sling that was pulling a cannonball out of a boiling pit of tar. The candle which was setting the weapon ablaze was near the door where Moshe stood.

The two men noticed Moshe standing tall in the doorway, his right leg scorched black. The man closest to Moshe looked up from the cannonball with a shocked look on his face. The realization that the intruder he was trying to stop had reached him sunk in quickly as he dropped his end of the sling and reached for his sword.

The second man was pulled down by the cannonball in the sling dipping both arms up to the elbows into the boiling tar. He screamed in pain as he felt and watched the skin on his arms bubble off the bone.

As the first man attempted to engage Moshe, he was met with the heavy shredded ball of the mace. The shotput sized sphere struck the man in the forearm crushing the ulna, hooking the skin and tearing it away faster than he could move the now throbbing arm. The sword flew from the man's hand to the wall, clanging in the background of the screams. The mace flung off to the side splattering the blood across the walls.

Moshe looked out at the men bloodied and left in torturous pain. The second man holding his broken arm hoping to stop the pain of his shredded skin. His voice wavered as he croaked out in disbelief, "Which king do you serve?"

"The king of all men. God." Moshe stated with a straight voice. He kicked the candle over into the vat of tar setting it ablaze along with the man kneeling next to it watching his arms melt away.

Moshe turned to continue his trek up the stairs as he heard the screams of the men muffle into choking as the thick spicy scent of tar and burning flesh chased Moshe up the stairs. His mind remained locked on his target as he stomped up each step. The thick smoke started to invade his lungs and burn his eyes. He began gasping for air just as he came to an opened window frame. He leaned out the into the fresh air to refill his lungs and escape the death smoke.

Looking out over the east side of the palace Moshe could see that the outer wall had completely fallen on that side and it appeared as though the fighting had died down. The lands were not filled with men slicing and burning each other anymore other than the sporadic fight all he could see were men, women and children coming to each other's aid.

The sight of such community warmed his heart and reminded him of why it was he had sieged on the castle. He turned back into the spire and returned to walking up the stairs. The smoke mostly poured out the open window making the rest of the journey up breathable.

As he pushed his way up the pain of the journey began to take its toll. His lungs coughed, his muscles ached, and his leg throbbed with the stinging burn. But as he put more and more weight on his staff and the mace clanked against each stair dragging behind him, his eyes came level with the top step. He pushed through the pain and reached the summit.

At the top step the stairs gave way to a landing that was decorated with golden furniture and lavish rugs and drapes. There was a tremendous bed with purple and yellow sheets. There was a balcony that opened up in six places and wrapped around the entire spire. Moshe could see the yellow king standing out on the balcony looking down at his kingdom in chaos.

Moshe limped over to the balcony dragging his mace behind him. The sky still lit with the explosion shined down reflecting against the bulbous golden topper above them on the spire.

The yellow king turned and looked at Moshe. His yellowed washed out skin sagged in too many places giving the impression that his mood was displayed across his skin. He looked back down at the palace, "I always feared I would be king when you came." The yellow king's voice was soft and wispy. "The prophecy was something that struck fear in my heart and I think unlike the other kings I knew it was for my time. I thought if I instilled violence in my subjects I would be unreachable, but I can't stop prophecy. It is meant to be."

He turned to Moshe and held his hands out to his side prepared for death. Moshe looked at him angry that he had to be the bringer of death.

"Will you recant your claim that you are of the only class that can speak to God, relinquish your rule over the grey people of this world, and recommit your life to the one true God?" The words came out in a low monotone.

The yellow king turned his face to the sky and spoke, "I denounced God as a birthright. There is no turning back for me."

Moshe swung the mace with all the strength he had left connecting with the skull of the yellow king. A crushing sound emitted like a window being shattered under a soaked sheet. The king drew in a final breath which emitted a type of gurgle which made Moshe gag. He let go of the mace of which its barbs stayed lashed onto the king's face. The blow pushed the man backwards and he toppled over the balcony. The persecution of the yellow king's rule ended with a cracking thud against the solid dirt below his chambers.

Chapter 15

Liberate

Maggie saw the yellow king fall to his death. She witnessed his head first dive into the ground splattering the dirt with a Rorschach inspired spot of blood. She knew that Moshe must be at the top of the spire from which the yellow king had fallen and she was desperate to find him.

She looked up the spire and saw him standing on the balcony. It seemed unimaginably high as if he was in the heavens. He spread his arms wide and screamed out, "I claim this land in the name of God for the grey people of this planet. For his people!"

Many of the people below raised a fist to the air and chanted in unison, "Hail the grey king."

Maggie started making her way into the spire, but as she began to ascend the stairs a grey man, young and fit, lightly pushed her aside and he began to run up the steps. He bounded three steps at a time and quickly was out of sight.

She panicked. The young man seemed to be heading somewhere with purpose and the idea that he may be on his way to slay the king killer was the only thing her mind would consider. She sped up, attempting to jump two and three steps at a time. It did not last long. She made it to the first room and panting from the exertion peeked in to find no one. She continued on, afraid of what may be happening at the top.

Her legs burned with activity and she wanted to quit, but her love was in danger so she pushed on. She reached the room with the tar vat and two deformed corpses. The sight and smell hit her at once and she vomited on the stones. She walked backwards out of the room and stumbled up the steps. Her stomach gurgled in anger as she tried to get the stench out of her nose and the taste out of her mouth. The vision was something she would live with forever, two men with bodies half melted, their skin tarred black and showing partial bones, other parts of their body swelled with boils larger than a small chicken.

She stumbled up the steps trying to rid herself of the knowledge of the two men, but it only delved her into a thick black smoke that filled the passageway. Holding her breath and closing her eyes she scrambled up the steps, banging her knees against stones and scratching her nails down to bloody bits trying to move as quickly as possible. When she could not hold her breath any longer she opened her eyes to a painful burn. Still scrambling up the steps her lungs forced her to intake smoke. She was coughing and choking, but her need to help Moshe forced her on.

At the last second when she thought she was going to succumb to the lack of oxygen she landed on the step where the smoke trailed out the open window. She lay on the cold stone floor gasping and panting. She had never felt relief like that. The life filling force of the clean air was so shocking to her system that she continued to cough. Her eyes, still burning watered much of the soot out and allowed her to see again.

She forced herself back up and crawled up the last few sets of steps to reach the top of the stairs where she drew her dagger out of its leg sheath. She approached the ornate room with caution still squinting through the watery burning of her pupils.

When she came around the corner Moshe stood there embracing the young man. They held each other in such a life affirming manner that she dropped her dagger allowing it clang against the floor. She fell to her knees in exhaustion.

The men looked up at the sound the metal banging around the floor to see Maggie filthy and in tears from the stress. Moshe pulled away from the young man and went to his wife.

"Maggie?" Moshe started with a kind and loving tone. "I want you to meet Ash, my son."

She looked up at the young man through the tears in her eyes and reached out to him. Ash leaned down and embraced her as he would his own mother.

Maggie babbled out loud trying to clear her mind of the fear that had invaded. "Moshe, I thought you were dead. I thought your son was someone who meant to kill you. I couldn't get here fast enough, I thought I lost you."

Both the men told her it was ok. That everything was fine now.

She calmed down and pulled away from Ash. She smiled letting her sobs break through the façade. "I'm so happy to meet you." She managed to get out through the puffs of breath.

Ash smiled back at her and said, "I am too. And I am so happy for you and my father."

They hugged again now both crying with a newfound happiness.

Moshe embraced her again and the three of them sat on the floor of the king's quarters holding each other in love and victory.

The girls seemed to have lost track of time as the daylight came on fast and appeared to be never ending. The daylight brought some good as it allowed them to see around the deck of the ship they were on. In addition to the bucket and rags there was three trunks full of shirts and pants, a stone fire ring with a pot for cooking, a vent they could open, several piles of fish and some vegetables that were still days away from rotting.

Wyndsoria had taken to caring for the whole bunch of girls. She helped Patricka rest trying to overcome the headache and hangover she still had. She got to know Ruthie and what her past looked like. She heard the story of meeting Ash on more than one occasion. She had come to love Ruthie in her own way and managed to treat the cruel experience forced upon them as a bad dream. She also spent a lot of time with Ruby. Much of it was helping the girl breathe through a trouble spot in her pregnancy, but once she got past that they spent time cooking fish together and calming Patricka down when panic struck her.

The tilting of the ship got to them all at some points, but they knew this was temporary. There was a destination they were headed to although Wyndsoria had conveniently forgotten.

Ruby had tried to break the news to her. Hoping that a small reminder might jog her memory, but with the simple idea of asking where she thought Ash might be she was greeted with a simple shrug. Either Wyndsoria had truly pushed it out of her mind or her sanity was just keeping the information at bay.

Ruby did her best to comfort and help Wyndsoria, but that was not her place in the relationship. Ruby was the one who needed the coddling and Wyndsoria was to be the strong one. It did not bother Wyndsoria as she had always been a strong woman. It was the biggest issue in her relationship with Moshe. She held men in a regard that made them strong and infallible. Her view of women was that of fragile and perfect creatures. She could care for a woman, but she couldn't take care of man.

Her connection with Ruby confused her at times. She felt so much in love with the woman, but it wasn't a physical desire that led that love. It was a mental connection. It was as if she felt less lonely with her. As if they were both apart of the same jigsaw puzzle.

Both Wyndsoria and Ruby rummaged through the trunks to find more clothes for everyone as they were dripping with sea mist in their current outfits. As Wyndsoria leaned into a trunk Ruby came up behind her and slid her arms over Wyndsoria's. The touch was subtle, but passionate for both of them.

Wyndsoria looked back at the pregnant girl and tried to smile. The movement cracked her scabs and let out small pinpoints of blood causing the battered woman to wince and whimper.

Ruby kissed the woman as lightly as possible and said to her as she pushed the hair out of her face, "Be strong. We will get you through this."

Wyndsoria smiled again, reaggravating the fresh wounds. A tear formed in her eye as she never felt so loved.

Moshe stood in front of the map of the world pleading to God to show him how their message had spread throughout the rest of the kingdoms. Having the map and planning area outside under the sunlight made him feel like he should have a better connection with God. But, no matter what he said, the map remained blank. Maggie held his arm trying to comfort him, but the idea that God had abandoned him and his people was a stab to the heart.

Dozens of people were gathered expecting to see the movements of the message to help determine where they should go to finalize their mission. Moshe was embarrassed and distraught.

He turned to face the group to try and explain that it appeared they were on their own, but Ash put his hand on his father's shoulder. He whispered into his ear, "Let me give it a shot." Ash stepped in front of map next to his father. "They need to believe this is coming from you. Go through the motions."

Ash stepped to the side a bit while his father raised his hands and asked aloud for the lord to show his people the movement of their message. At the same time, Ash quietly spoke to God asking for guidance. The map sprung to life with grey lights littering the terrains. There were no red, black, or yellow lights left. The white kingdom remained mostly white, but the brightest white light sparkled in the middle of the ocean between the white and yellow kingdoms. They watched as the sparkling light drifted closer and closer to the yellow kingdom where they now stood.

Once it arrived a single grey dot met the sparkling white dot and the entire map went dark. Moshe turned to face the group and said, "It appears our missionary work is mostly done. We must spread to the white kingdom, but only after their messenger arrives here." The words were met with an indifference that he did not expect. The group was hesitant of the sparkling white light having seen the entire map go dark. The confidence Moshe tried to portray did not extend to the rest of the group.

Ash walked away from the planning area and into one of the small weapon rooms that were randomly scattered throughout the yellow palace. Moshe and Maggie followed him as the crowd had already started to disperse.

Moshe looked at his son, "What happened back there? God used to speak to me."

Ash looked his father in the eye and with a smile, "I think you passed it on to me. A few days ago, I spoke with God and I understand now that it is our family that can speak to God. You have passed the ability down to me. I think you might have given it up for me."

"But, my father didn't give me the ability." Moshe was skeptical about the idea.

"Because he wasn't your birth father." Ash looked at Maggie who was now holding her hand over her mouth.

Moshe furrowed his brow trying to piece together the message his son was trying to tell him. "You mean we are blood?"

Ash let his emotions explode on his face, smiling all the way across his jaw.

Moshe looked at his son for a moment, "But how?"

"I was told that God influenced the world to assure we were placed together. To help bring the prophecy to the world. The prophecy of our family overthrowing the kings."

Moshe grabbed his son and hugged him as if it would be the last time. They shared an embrace that transcended generations. It was the embrace of an entire lineage reuniting. It seemed to last an eternity, but eventually they each pulled back from their hug.

Moshe cleared his throat, "Ok, we need to prepare for this final sparkling messenger."

Chapter 16

Final Stand

Eventhough there was light coming in from between the boards of the ship, when the crew opened the door and the sunlight came in unfiltered the intensity of the light was painful to all the women. They blocked the pain as best they could with their hands, but none of them could really see.

The king and his men came in and forcefully removed the women from their holding deck.   There was no gentleness, they grabbed them and loaded them onto a dingy treating them as nothing more than cargo.

The king watched each of the women as they were unloaded from their cell. He muttered insults to himself for each of the women, calling Patricka useless, Ruthie a whore, and Ruby a waste of beauty. But, when Wyndsoria was dragged past him he said nothing. He only smiled at the swollen bloodied face that he knew was his own doing.

Once the girls were loaded onto a dingy, the king and his guards boarded it as well and they lowered themselves into the ocean. In the small boat was the king, two rowing guards, the four women and one guard assigned to each one of them.

The women and their captors sat in the center of the rowboat being held in place with their arms behind their backs.

The king looked towards the shore with a somber look on his face. This was his final stand and he was becoming more and more aware of his fate. As they rowed closer to the shore of the yellow kingdom he could see that the perimeter wall of the palace had been destroyed. There was obviously an attack on the capital city.

Everything started to make sense. The forgotten, although he thought had been sent to the fat kingdom to rot away in a prison cell, was actually in his castle the whole time. Ash was the forgotten, went to the yellow kingdom and usurped the king. Unless Ash had truly been acting on his king's behalf, this was his final march. He was a dead man walking.

He looked back at the women and realized that if the prophecy was true he was dead already. But, it did not mean he couldn't face Ash and kill everyone he loved. He was ready for death, but he was taking the four women with him.

The boat slowly pushed through the water bobbing up and down as the waves passed their progress. The image of the palace was becoming more clear. The walls had fallen and the flag of the Penta Diamond had been removed. In its place flew a solid grey flag. He felt it was proof that Ash had taken the city for himself.

As they came close to land, the waves began to break and the spray from the ocean hit them as they sat. The king breathed in the thick salty sea air for what he assumed would one of the last times.

The boat ran aground. The king disembarked first with a guard flanked to each side. The four guards followed with their captives. They sloshed through the shallow waters looking at the amazing feat of destruction that lay before them. The wall of the city was close enough to see that it was destroyed beyond their original impression. It was not just torn down, but burnt as well. They could see large amounts of people milling around the palace grounds behind where the wall should be.

The king stopped when he noticed a group of grey men walking from the palace down towards them. It did not take long for him to recognize Ash, the four men and the woman that came with were mysteries to him.

The king turned his back to the approaching group. He looked out onto the waters, gazing at the two now abandoned ships drifting in front of the building storm that was pushing a cold breeze towards the beach. The sounds of the storm clashed and whipped across the waters pushing the waves farther up the shore. He took a deep breath and ordered his guards, "Swords out. I want blades at throats, slice if they charge."

He turned back as the group approached.

Ash led the way with Moshe close behind him. Buz and Loht flanked Maggie as they did not like the idea of her coming, but she would not leave Moshe's side.

Ash stopped when they were fifty feet away. He stared at the swords pressed against the throats of his mother, sister, and love. He tried to not show panic. Instead he walked the rest of the distance alone and bowed to the king, "My lord."

The king swiftly unsheathed his sword and swung with a mighty force at the neck of young Ash. Ash pivoted in the sand swinging his head to the side allowing the king's sword to strike the beach.

Ash took a few steps back as he spoke again, "I guess that ruse is unnecessary."

The king laughed as he retracted the sword from the sand, "I don't understand. Go ahead, bow to your king again." A wicked grin flashed across the king's face.

Ash still walking backward turned to face Moshe and

bowed deeply hoping to get the ire of the king up.

A low growl came from the royal man as he charged towards Ash, sword straight forward as a spear. Ash spun out of the way then drew his own sword as the king spun around to face his foe.

The two men circled, swords up, as the wind began to pick up force and small spittle of rain started to fall. Ash would not remove his eyes from the king's gaze, "You know how this ends. Why fight it? The prophecy says you will not kill me."

The king swung his sword at the young man, just to have it deflected by his target's sword. "Poor Ash. Maybe I cannot kill you. Maybe you will have my head before the day is done, but nowhere is it written that I won't slice the throats of your mother, sister, and whore before you are forced to watch them bleed to death on this beach."

The king leered back at the women teasing Ash, deciding which of the women he would give the command to have killed first. Moshe couldn't watch he reached for his staff, but the light of God appeared against his chest and held him in place.

The appearance of the light put the king's men on high alert, they also tried to draw their weapons, but the light of God spread and kept everyone at bay. No one could move, but the king and Ash.

The king looked at his men wrapped in a shimmering sheath of boundaries. He retreated to his side and looked at the crowd. He ordered his men to step forward, but they did not budge. He walked over to Wyndsoria and slapped her across the broken side of her face. She screamed out in agony, but did not budge. "What is this force of evil?" The king screamed out looking at Ash accusingly.

"This is not evil. This is the lights of God. He is allowing the prophecy to be fulfilled. It is me against you."

Ash responded and then charged the king with his sword raised above his head.

The king leapt up striking his own sword against Ash's forcing the blade backwards almost knocking Ash on his back. The king landed and quickly spun to his right holding the sword outstretched. Ash ducked the first swipe and on the king's second rotation he planted his own sword in the ground creating a pole that stopped the king's spin and the ring of metal on metal shocked the royal hand.

The king tossed the sword to his left hand shaking out the right from the sting. As he blocked various strikes from Ash he taunted his foe. "Moments after you left Jaso told me you made the stars move at night." He flipped the sword back to his right hand, thrusting jabs towards Ash in two quick motions. "That was when it hit me that you may be the forgotten and I may have just sent you off to fulfill the prophecy." Ash jabbed back at the king which he sidestepped and deflected with a quick upward swing.

The winds picked up chilling the bodies of everyone in the area. Ash ran to the side and blocked multiple low attacks that endangered his feet and ankles. "So, then why are you fighting it? God told me that he would not let me die by the hand of man. You are only delaying your defeat."

The king spat towards the former guard and walked backwards towards the women. He stood behind Ruthie putting his sword to her neck and his other arm around her waist. "You are right, Ash. I should just kill her right now so you can be a hero to all the world except your wasted whore!" He slid his left hand up the girl's stomach and squeezed her breast with a violent and strong grip.

"No! What do you want?" Ash screamed out dropping his sword in a sort of physical begging.

"I want you to denounce your God. I want you to cry out that you forsake your place in prophecy and fight me one on one so I can kill you like the worthless child you are."

Ash knelt down, grabbed his sword and pointed it to the sky. "God, I am no longer your servant. I beg of you to release me from your prophecy and allow whoever you deem to be next to become the forgotten. Do not protect me from death by the hand of man. And let me battle the king on an equal footing." As the words left his lips lightning stuck one of the king's ships that were bobbing just off the coast in the ocean. The rain began to pour down on the two men as if God had responded to the request.

The king was satisfied with the signs and grabbed Ruthie by the jaw and kissed her deep and hard. The move had the desired effect on Ash as he sprang to his feet and rushed the king with his sword pointed straight ahead. The king released the girl and jumped to the side deflecting Ash's sword nearly into Ruthie's chest.

The shock of nearly murdering the woman he loved made Ash stop in panic. The moment took the energy out of him and he dropped to his knees sliding on the wet sand.

The king spun around and swung his sword overhead and brought it down to where Ash knelt. The boy moved seconds before his skull was cracked by the king's sword. He scrambled to his feet and dashed away towards the captive group of people who had accompanied him to the battle.

The king chased after Ash swinging and not connecting with anything but beach sand. When Ash turned to face the king again they both swung their swords creating a volley of clanging metal as they traded blows and blocks.

Ash noticed the king lifting his sword leaving himself vulnerable and he kicked his former ruler knocking the man onto his back sliding slightly into the sand. Ash pushed his body and swung three times at the king with all his power, but the king rolled out of the way each time. The white king returned to his feet and slashed at Ash's abdomen. It was blocked, but the rain had coated the boys hand so much that his sword slipped from his grip.

The king tried to take advantage by thrusting toward Ash, but he missed by inches each time as Ash dodged and evaded the blade. Ash saw an opportunity and tackled the king knocking the sword from his hand as well.

Ash had the upper hand and half mounted the king who laid on his back. The boy sent punch after punch to the face of the king splattering blood across the man's robes. The rain poured so heavily that Ash had to wipe the water out of his eyes, but in that moment the king took advantage of the momentary slip and out of desperation slapped Ash square in the Adam's apple.

The boy twisted back and removed himself from the king while he grasped at his throat in the shock of not being able to breath. It only lasted half a second then both men scrambled to retrieve their swords.

The king attacked again and another volley of swipes occurred filling the beach with the classic sounds of swordfight. Ash ducked away and then charged the king and once again they traded blocks. But, as the king turned to escape the stalemate of attacks Ash caught the him in the shoulder.

It was not a mortal wound, but a small scratch. The king looked over at his shoulder and saw the blood. The sight and sensation of the cut angered him. He grabbed a handful of dirt and launched it into the face of Ash momentarily blinding the boy.

As Ash tried to block the attack with his sword, but he was left cleaning his eyes with his hand and the rain. The king retreated back behind Patricka. He pointed his blade at her chest as he screamed through the storm at Ash. "Your little sister was useless in her calling! A waste of space in my castle."

Ash could see again and turned to face the king who sidestepped down the line to Wyndsoria where his sword taunted her throat. "You mother's face was mutilated into what you see now by me and the wall of my quarters."

Ash snorted in anger and started walking towards the king who sidestepped again to Ruthie where held the blade at her stomach. Ash stopped at the threat of Ruthie being victim to the king.

The king smiled as he slowly positioned himself to where Ash could see him perfectly and the girl was in line to receive a sword through the abdomen. "This little whore here is going to die because of you." He watched as Ash tried to compose himself. "After seeing you galivant this tramp around my kingdom without any modesty or a shred of cloth to cover her up, I had to see what the fuss was about."

Ash began to shake his head in defiance of belief. "I took her from you. I had her. I have had every part of her, she wanted me, she felt me in her, I have made her do things she will never forget. Things that will make her tremble for years to come."

Ash screamed back, "No! Shut up!"

The king laughed, "Then I made another have her. Your own mother has had the sweet sensation that is your little bitch Ruthie."

Ash refused to believe it, but when he saw the tears well up in Ruthie's eyes and his mother start to sob he understood it was true. He couldn't charge the king, he couldn't make a move if he wanted to save Ruthie. So, he dropped to his knees. He dropped his sword and let his shoulders go limp in defeat.

"You pathetic waste of a man. Know that I am your king. I am the ruler of all you horrible creatures. I take what I want and you take what I give you. You may have God on your side who won't release you from your duty as the forgotten. He won't let me kill you by my hand, but I can kill you in other ways." The king pulled the sword back and began to thrust for Ruthie's gut.

Ash reached out from his knees trying to touch her one last time before she was skewered. As his heart stopped and the world seemed to slow, a lightning bolt stuck the sword the king held and threw the king, his guards and the women dozens of feet in every direction.

Sparks shot up out of the ground as the bolt struck the king's sword with a blinding force. The light of God dissipated and everyone could move again. Ash ran to the side of his love asking her if she was ok, petting her hair and cradling her neck.

Once Moshe realized that he was free to move he walked over to the fallen king. He knelt down beside the man and retrieved his sword. The king had one eye that appeared to be stuck in place while the other swiveled around madly looking at the world around him. His arm had a strange scribble pattern across it alongside what appeared to be some instantaneous burn marks.

Moshe leaned in close to the man, "I have been serving God my entire life. You tried to stop that. You tried to have me removed from my family and destroyed. You tried to destroy my son. And you are the only life I wanted to take during this whole ordeal." He stood up and thrust the sword down into the chest of the king.

Epilogue

Wyndsoria, Ruby, and Patricka

Patricka kissed her mother before she ran off to school. It was still a strange experience as her face looked normal, but Patricka could still feel the scars when she kissed her cheek. As she turned to sprint out the door Ruby cried out, "She gets a kiss and I don't?" Patricka sulked over to her other mother and gave her a peck on the cheek. She felt it was bad enough that an eleven year old has to kiss her mom goodbye, but her new mom as well.

She turned and ran out the door of their apartment. Ruby walked over to Wyndsoria and gave her a big hug. Wyndsoria sighed as she worried about their daughter walking alone through the streets to get to school.

Ruby gave Wyndsoria a kiss to break her concentration. "You know this isn't the same city it was."

Wyndsoria shook her head, "I know, I know. Sodorrah is no more, it is now the city of Abrael."

Ruby laughed at the comment, "No. I mean the bath houses are gone, the palace has been opened up for worship, faith in God has overtaken the city. This isn't even the capital anymore. Patricka is just as safe going to school here as she was when you were back in Listerbourne."

She nodded her agreement and walked over to the closet. She put on her medical robes in preparation for work.

Ruby looked over at her and thought about the lost child. She thought it every time she watched her love go off to work. But, that morning she decided to finally say something. "When you are at work and helping women deliver babies so they can go home and live with their birth child," She paused as she looked at her feet in discomfort. "Do you ever wish my child would have survived? Do you wish that we could live our lives with another baby?"

She turned back and held the woman in her arms. "I have all I need. You and Patricka. But, I think it was a blessing from God that the child didn't survive. The child of the white king? How could anyone live with that hovering over them for their entire life? What if it was born white instead of grey? No, I think the heartache you and I have felt losing a child is more bearable than the heartache we would feel if we were the caretakers of the king's child."

Ruby laid her head down on Wyndsoria's shoulder and rejoiced in the fact that she was safe, loved, and happy. It was a mutual feeling. Wyndsoria had never felt such a part of a family as she did with Patricka and Ruby. She needed to get to work, but standing there with Ruby felt more important at the moment.

Ash and Ruthie

The former land of the red king had been quite a change for Ash and Ruthie. The weather was humid, the plant life was lush with green foliage, and the animals that prowled were more dangerous than back at home.

Ash had just finished speaking to the people of Edihn about the mission he and his father had received from God. He explained how they were free, the importance of looking to the divine for help and how they should never return to the worship of man over God.

The message was an easy one to get across as the red and black kings both fell with without a central figure present during the uprisings. The people of those kingdoms were eager to accept God.

Ash stepped off the stage and walked over to the group of women Ruthie was talking to. She looked up and saw her husband and happily lifted their three month old son over her head so he would take the baby.

He held his son and thanked him as he always did. After the death of the last king, the white king, they wondered why God intervened. The prophecy had no mention of God saving Ruthie. A few month later when they learned they were pregnant. That is when it became clear that when Ash asked God to pass on the prophecy of the forgotten, it was passed on to the child recently conceived between Ash and Ruthie. It was he, who would eventually be born Emmanuel that could not be killed by the hand of man and therefore was saved by God when the king had planned to kill his mother.

"If any of you need someone to talk to please come and find us. We will be in your town until the next full moon." Ruthie concluded her meeting with the women of the town. She had taken her experiences with the king and used them as a building block to help others throughout the world who had trouble coming to terms with their past in the old world of the kings.

She stood and embraced her husband happy to be doing something for humanity. She kissed him and grabbed his hand. She was prepared to drag him back to their tent where they were staying until they moved on to the next town. Their time in the towns was often spent with others. Their family time was short and rare. Anytime Ruthie saw the opportunity to be away she seized it.

But, before they removed themselves from the town square a young boy came up to them. He kept glancing back at the man and woman standing a few dozen feet behind him, watching him approach his prince and princess.

He looked up at the couple and said in a soft six year old voice, "Excuse me. Grey princess?"

Ruthie kneeled down to talk to the boy at his level.

"Is it true that you can talk to God?" The boy looked at Ruthie which such innocence and interest that it nearly melted her heart.

Ruthie patted the boy on the head, "We can all talk to God. But, Prince Ash here used to hear God's replies."

"Do you hear it anymore?"

Ash looked down at the boy smiling, "No, but Emmanuel hears him now." He holds up his son so the boy can see who he was talking about.

The boy's eyes lit up with excitement. "What does he sound like?"

"Like all the love in the world speaking to your heart in a single moment."

The boy looked down, unimpressed with the description. He looked back at Ruthie, "Princess Ruthie, you are beautiful." He gave the princess a peck on the cheek and ran back to his parents in the square.

The couple chuckled to themselves and walked back to their tent.

Moshe and Mary Maggie

Loht stood in the darkness in the corner of the room. He was not used to the small town life of Listerbourne, but he would follow his king anywhere. They stood in Moshe's office in the church where representatives to the government continuously appeared asking Moshe for his guidance in how to properly take care of the people.

Maggie also stood back in the shadows watching her husband and king explain to the men who devoted their new lives to running the government that everything they do is for the benefit of mankind. There should be nothing that harms anyone coming from their work.

She was always happy to watch her husband speak on his passions and his passions were God and his people.

As the government men took their orders and walked away Father Fairow appeared in the doorway. He had become Moshe's apprentice. Under the tutelage of the king he was learning just how to best communicate the word of God as understood from a man who had truly heard the voice of God.

Maggie understood that it was going to be long discussion between the two priests as they prepared for the service in the morning. She tapped Loht on the shoulder and they walked down the stairs together. When they got outside they watched the sun setting over the horizon. They saw the children play in the street while the market, blacksmith shop, and butchery closed up for the night and the workers start their trek home. It was a nice picture. It was everything that should have always been and finally was.

If you enjoyed this book or would like to support
me, please consider leaving a rating or review. It really helps
me out as well as those looking for something to read.

Reviews or ratings at

Amazon.com

Goodreads.com

BookDNA.com

Bn.com

Or where ever you buy or talk about books

Just look for Richard W. Kelly

Fantasy Casting

I've tried to make it a staple of my books to fantasy cast them into movies. It is a fun activity where I get to talk a little about how I feel about the characters and compare them to actors that I appreciate.

So, this is the fantasy cast for Kings of One Color.

Moshe - As far as Moshe is concerned. It needs someone who can be thoughtful and a leader. Someone who can be reserved and not want to fulfill their duties. I really like Brendan Hunt from Ted Lasso. He is a bit quiet in the show, but I like the feel he has on screen.

Wyndsoria - No question Elisabeth Moss. Huge fan of her work in A Handmaid's Tale and I think that Wydsoria is a similar character at times. She is likely more opportunistic, but the same bold rebel if for different reasons.

Patricka - I'm at a loss here. I made the character too young to cast. I think she would have to make her an early teen. then I could go with Alexa Swinton. Saw her recently in Old and was very impressed.

Ash - This part to me is the guy that is coming into his own and learns to not be selfish. Nick Robinson caught my attention in a fun, but ridiculous film, Shadow in the Cloud. I think his work there fits here.

White King - This role needs someone who is someone of a sleaze bag. Someone who can be pompous and gross, but also charming and responsible. I am thinking Luke Kirby. Love his portrayal of Lenny Bruce and I think he has that dark perverse side in him somewhere.

Ruthie - This is a worn down girl. Someone with such dreams, but knows they are already gone. Someone shy, but willing. Peyton Kennedy from Everything Sucks feels like a solid choice. A show that Netflix needs to resurrect BTW.

Mary - Someone meek and quiet, but enough of a presence to bear a huge destiny. I think of Sarah Levy. There is something about her work on Schitt's Creek that accomplishes both the shy and bold.

Author's Note

It took a long time to finish this book. It is one that I can officially say this book took me three years to write, but that really isn't true. This book was half written in the end of 2013 and finished in January of 2017.

I don't know what happened, but at some point I lost the motivation for it and over the three years that I left it unfinished the story continued to evolve in my head. I don't know that it would have turned out the same had I finished it back then.

The book was born of a single idea. "If everyone's background was so intertwined and the average person was just a mix would the few who had non-diverse ancestry be revered or hated?" It grew into something completely different after that question, but one basics of it remained.

This book was written with the writing process of Orson Scott Card in mind. I read his book How to Write Science Fiction and Fantasy when I was seventeen years old. The process has been in the back of mind since. Over the years I tried to utilize different processes for writing stories and books. The first time I tried to use Card's process was when I wrote the short story "Kings of One Color" which is collected in my book Solundrums.

That was the most planning I ever did for a story. I spent months planning out characters and histories and maps and governments… In the end I loved the short story, but there was so much left out. So, back in 2011 when I wrote it I shelved all the extra stuff as something for another story.

In 2013 I used Stephen King's writing process that he wrote about in On Writing. It got me half way through The Psi-Chotic Adventures of Drew Darby, then I had to stop and switch to my own process. I think the same thing happened here. I tried to use Card's process, but it stalled out for me half way through.

From here on out it is my own process, which appears to involve following someone else's until I get stuck.

A Preview of Another Tale

It took a long time to move onto my next book. It is probably due to the idea that I had not been very successful at this point. I was starting to see how much time it was taking to write and how little came out of it. I continued to write the occasional short story, but I took a long break from serious writing.

The Early Years of 'Squirt' Malone came out in 2022, over five years after Kings of One Color. Just like Kings, Squirt started out as a short story about the carnival years of wrestling.

I am a big wrestling fan, especially the history of it. To the point that I had considered a coffee table book about the original world title. I think that passion helped me step back into writing while paying attention to a subject that I hold very dear to me.

So, this is a preview of The Early Years of 'Squirt' Malone, a historical fiction about the early years of wrestling.

Before it All Began

I wish that I could recall what my early childhood was like. Maybe if I had written my memoirs when I was thirty I could have remembered, but this old brain does not recall anymore. I was born at the turn of the century, in fact, I was considered a new year's baby. Born January the first in eighteen hundred ninety-eight, the year of our lord. My father owned a ranch in Denton County, Texas. I was one of eight children. I had four brothers and three sisters. I landed somewhere in the middle.

I spent a lot of time in my youth raising cattle because that is what our family did. We raised cattle and sold them off to butchers, rodeos, farms, boot makers… I learned a lot in those days, but little of it stuck with me. I guess my connection to animals remained and if I had not worked with cows all those years I probably would not have been able to steal a horse at twelve and start my life. But, that is getting ahead.

I did not go to school much. I went on occasion and so did my brothers. I think our father thought that one of us might make something of ourselves, but he needed too many hands on the ranch to let us all go. We sort of traded off. I probably spent a couple months a year going to class. I learned how to read, how to do my arithmetic, and some basics civics. My sisters tended the calves and helped mama with the house. They did not have a chance in this world, but back then, they just dreamed of marrying well.

I also worked for Denton Record Chronicle in the winter months when the cattle prices were down. Less demand, you know. The winter did not have butchers and farmers competing with the rodeos and cattle drivers for available cattle. If I was not learning or tending to the herd, I was either in the town square trying to sell papers or hanging around the telegraph office waiting to hear about the wrestling matches.

I had an obsession with wrestling. There was something about the clash of two powerhouses putting one another into impossible positions and using both their physical dominance and their intelligence to out maneuver their opponent.

In 1907, a carnival came to town. It was the first time we had a carnival stop in Denton. We were one of the bigger counties in the state, but the town of Denton had maybe four thousand folks that were close enough to actually go to the carnival. More showed up than you would have thought, more showed up than the carnival folks had thought.

They did not stop because they thought it was a good place to make some money, but because there was damage to the old Kansas-Missouri-Texas rail line. It was a couple days before the line would be fixed and the carnies just figured they had set up the tent and make some money.

It is one of my first memories. I was just nine years old and I remember the whole family making the hike to the fairgrounds. It was one of the only times I remember the whole family going somewhere together. It was not the same back then, you did not just up and leave very often. There were things to be done and animals to be tended to. So, that carnival was a special treat that children today would not understand.

I can still feel the dust in the hot summer wind making me squint my eyes as I watched the big red tent come into view as we trudged across the university campus to reach the fairgrounds. It was a couple hour walk that would have been twenty minutes on horse, but we did not have five horses to take us all. I could not believe the size of the tent, I could see it from a mile away. The excitement built within my belly and I got more and more giddy until we reached the edge of the grounds where they had a humongous sign that we walked under that read 'Johnny J. Jones Exposition - The greatest feats of man under one tent, one midway, and one spectacle for the entire family'.

It was kind of like Christmas to me. I spent so much of my time working and learning when you got a chance to just have fun, it was special. Outside of Christmas where we got a new toy and a morning where pops did all the work this is the only memory I have of a moment in that family where we were all having a grand time.

I remember pops handing me four quarters. I had never held so much money. He assigned one of my sisters to stick with me. I can still hear his gravelly voice, "That money best last you both all day. I came here to see the show in the big top and play some midway games. The Wild West show is in the big tent around sundown and is a dime an entry. If you waste your money you will have to sit outside the tent and wait for us."

When those words disappeared into the scuttle of people and ring of the calliope, he dropped those coins into my hands and rubbed his heavy calloused hand across my forehead tousling my hair in the process. I drug my older sister, Mazy, with me as I took off down the dirt path between the shoddily made booths and small tents.

We went overboard. The amount of food we ate, the games we played, and the sideshows we saw. It was a glorious day for my childhood. Mazy and I shared a humongous turkey leg. I swear the thing was bigger than my head. But, I think most things back then seemed large.

But, nothing was as large as Farmer Slate. When I was questioning whether or not to spend a nickel trying to get into the hootchie dance show, I noticed a circle of people rooting someone on just past the tent. I walked over trying to see over the spectators when a man suddenly stood up. He towered over the crowd of people watching. He was tall and muscular which he had on display only wearing a pair of tight pants and boots. His hair was a mess and matched his thick and unruly mustache. He laughed in a deep powering rumble claiming that he pinned his opponent in less than ten seconds.

As I reached the edge of the circle of spectators, I could see another man, much younger, much smaller crawling away from the scene.

"Any other takers? Spend one minute with me Andrew the Farmer Slate without getting pinned and win fifty green backs." The man said as he slowly turned in a circle with arms spread wide.

Eventually, I would come to learn that the Farmer was at the end of his career. And even though I had heard tales of his matches with Tom Stat, Billy Mulders, and Geoffrey Dubois, he was well past his prime. Just a few months prior to my meeting him, he had lost back-to-back matches to Fred Gottlieb and never rebounded.

But, at the time, I did not understand what an out of shape wrestler looked like. In my head, the man in that dirt circle beating up kids twenty years younger than him was a living God.

I stepped forward looking at the giant.

"Costs a dollar kid." Mr. Slate looked down at me expecting me to take him on. I just shook my head and tried to mumble my awe and inspiration to him. He patted me on the head and pushed me out of the way to see if he had any other takers past me.

I watched for hours as he manhandled teens and young twenty-somethings taking each boy's dollar as he made him groan and scream in agony. After all the bravery had left the men and boys at the fair and the Farmer knew he wasn't making any more money for the day he knelt down next to me and handed me a small piece of paper with an address on it.

"Squirt, I see the look in your eyes." He did not know it, but he just gave me a name. "That's the same way I looked at wrestlers when I was young. That address there is mine. I have a workout program that will help you get to where you need to be in the next ten years to try and do what I do. Send me twenty-five dollars and your address and I will send you the program."

The rest of that day is a blur to me. I think it was a blur when it happened also. My mind was so awestruck by a real life grappler that I did not know how to handle it. My sister ate ice cream and saw the gorilla show while I just waited patiently for her.

Even at the end of the night when everyone met back at the big red tent, I claimed I spent all my money and waited for the family. I already had it in my head that I was going to send off for that correspondence package.

I missed out on the Wild West show. From what I heard about it on the walk home and the research I have done in the rest of my life, I believe it to have been a knock off

Wild Bill's show. But sitting on the dirt listening to what was happening on the other side of the tent, I could not have been more at peace.

I might have been the only non-carny out there. But, I watched the sunset while the carnival folks packed things up, shard some spirits, and collected their day's pay.

The walk home took twice as long, partially due to the lack of sunlight, partially due to our feet hurting. It did not matter to me, I was trying to devise a plan where I could make twenty-five dollars and start my journey to becoming a professional wrestler.